THE DESERT PILOT/ VALLEY OF JEWELS

LEISURE BOOKS  NEW YORK CITY

A LEISURE BOOK®

October 1997

Published by special arrangement with
Golden West Literary Agency.

Dorchester Publishing Co., Inc.
276 Fifth Avenue
New York, NY 10001

ISBN 0-8439-4315-7

Printed in the United States of America.

THE DESERT PILOT

1

Pegasus and the Ox

One step beyond Billman lay the desert; young Ingram, minister of the Gospel, took the single step and sat down in the shadow of a rock amid the wilderness. Already one needed the shadow; for though the sun was barely above the horizon – had lost the rose and gold of dawn only the moment before – it was now white with strength and flooded the desert with a scorching heat. When the knee of the Reginald Oliver Ingram projected into that heat, he withdrew it. It was as though a burning glass had been focused neatly on it. He looked down, half expecting to see the cloth of his trousers smoking. And this heat would increase until early afternoon, after which its power would diminish by almost imperceptible degrees. Until its face turned red, the sun would flood the desert with white fire.

Like shimmering snow was the face of that desert, except that snow is fixed and still, whereas the sands were covered with little wraiths and atmospheric lines. They quivered and throbbed, as a white-hot iron quivers and throbs. Mr. Ingram raised his eyes from the paper on his knee and took more careful stock of all that lay around him. He had been in Billman only a few days – not long enough to preach his first sermon, as a matter of fact – but he had come across the continent with a suitcase filled with books. From their well-studied contents he could name yonder gigantic saguaro, and the opuntias, surrounded with a halo of ivory sheen in the strong sunlight; and he knew also the deer-horn cactus not far off, the greasewood and mesquite on the sands.

To name all the living things in sight was to give an impression of companionable multitudes about him, but as a matter of fact all he observed was hardly more to the desert than is an occasional mist of white to the broad, pale bosom of the summer sky – nothing to give shadow, for the intense sun will look through the spectral clouds when it stands directly above them. So it was with this plant life – a few fantastic forms, looking like odd cartoons of animals, thrust in the sand with arms or legs extended foolishly – and yonder patches that looked like smoke against the sand.

But Mr. Ingram looked upon all these signs of desolation with an eye that was unafraid; for he carried about him a spiritual armor that blunted the edge of every danger and every painful instance: When he left the theological school, a wise, ancient and holy man had said to him: 'Now you are about to enter the world. Leave some of your books and bookishness behind you. Be a man among men; trust the angels a little less and man a little more!' The Reverend Reginald Ingram smiled as he thought of this speech. For, looking across the desert, it seemed to him that the hand of God was visibly revealed, and he penned hastily and strongly the first words of the sermon which he would deliver later that morning: 'Dear brothers and sisters whom I meet here at the edge of our civilization, we have gone very far from our old homes and we have left many of our old ideas behind us; we even have stepped beyond the reach of the law, I suppose; but we have not passed beyond the reach of God, and I wish to speak to you to-day concerning the signs of His loving Fatherhood which are scattered about us, though the signs are unregarded by most of us, I fear.'

Having finished this burst, he paused, knitting his brows with the farseeing effort of a poet or a prophet. He glanced then to the tall forms of the San Joaquin Mountains far to the north and east, now washed with tides of light through air so pure and thin and dry that he could see the shadows which the boulders cast and almost pick out the individual trees which straggled up to timber line. Beyond that line was a band of purple, and above the purple lay the glittering caps of snow and eternal ice which, like a cup of haunting coolness, were offered forever to the sight of the parched desert beneath. A gleam of wings near by drew his attention to the fluttering butterfly which wafted aimlessly up and down close to the sand, all jeweled and transparent in the powerful sun.

The rapid pencil of the Reverend Reginald Oliver Ingram ran again over the paper:

'Here, beyond the law, conscious of our own strength, and aware of the apparently cruel face of nature, we prepare ourselves for battle. But our Father in heaven permits life without battle, and sends out unarmed multitudes, who persist and give the earth gentleness and beauty. Consider the butterfly that flutters softly over the desert, harmless, soft, brilliant in the sun –'

He looked up for inspiration to complete his sentence, and noticed an active little cactus wren, balanced on a hideous thorn of the deer-horn plant.

'– or the wren,' dashed on the swift pencil of the minister, 'spreading his wings that the sun may flash through them and make of him a double jewel –'

He looked again, and saw almost at his feet a little yellow beetle looking as hard and glittering as a piece of quartz.

He touched it with the eraser of his pencil; it was, indeed, like pressing on a rock.

'– or the beetle,' went on the writer in glad haste, 'like a nugget of gold on the face of the desert. But these defenseless ones which can harm nothing and which give joy to the world teach us that we, also –'

Something whirred through the air; the butterfly was clipped in two by the long, wicked beak of the wren. The quivering halves tumbled almost at the feet of the watcher, but since he had sat quietly so long, the bird seemed to accept him as a part of the landscape, and pursuing its prey, gobbled up the feast and was gone.

Mr. Ingram looked down at his page and puckered his lips in thoughtful regret. However, he continued: 'Teach us that we, also, have been placed in the world to make it beautiful with the work of the heart and not terrible and dangerous with the work of the hand. Gentleness is mightier than pride –'

He paused again, and saw that the golden beetle had encountered a smaller insect. Whatever it might have been, it was now unrecognizable. For the yellow beauty, beating its shardlike wings with joy or anger, was already tearing the weaker thing to bits.

'Gentleness is mightier than pride,' insisted Mr. Ingram's pencil, 'and the triumphs of the strong are, in reality, not triumphs at all; they are soon avenged.'

He completed the sentence rather grimly, and another whir in the air attracted him once more to the wren, which had dropped like lightning from its bower of thorns and attacked the golden beetle.

There was no battle. The beetle depended on the toughness of its armor, and depended in vain, for soon Ingram could hear the crackling of this natural coat of plate, and the beetle presently disappeared. Thereafter, the wren flitted onto a stone, and sat there opening its beak wide, pulling in its head, and ruffling its feathers as though it found its recent tough meal very hard to digest.

'I hope you choke on it!' said the minister sternly to the bird. And he wrote: 'Vengeance is near at hand, and we are being watched by a higher power. The victories which we win are always just around the corner from defeat!'

So wrote the man of God, and he had barely finished this sentence when new ideas forced themselves upon him, and he added fluently: 'Put off your guns and knives! The God who rules heaven and earth is a God of peace. Trust to Him, and He will lead you out of your troubles. What blow can threaten you that He will not ward away?'

He felt a glow of triumphant conviction as he finished. At that instant he heard a hiss like a volley of arrows whirring above him; a shadow slanted with incredible speed past his head; the wren was blotted out; there was a shrill scream, and away winged the big hawk which had dropped from the blue – and now sailed back into it, carrying a little tuft of crimsoned feathers in one set of talons.

Ingram watched the bird of prey rising gracefully and rapidly, climbing the sky in great spirals. It reminded him of the men he had seen in Billman since his arrival – lean, quiet men, who, when they were roused to action, struck with sudden and deadly stroke. And all at once he felt more than a little helpless, for it seemed to him that he could hear the chuckles of his audience when he told them later that morning that there was no value in might or in the strong hand.

What lessons of gentleness could he derive from that nature where the smaller beetle was eaten by the larger, the larger by the wren, the wren by the hawk which towered in the sky, and the hawk, in turn, perhaps struck down by the soaring eagle? However, he would not be downhearted at once.

He followed the flight of the hawk past the cold summits of the San Joaquin range, and as he did so, the glory of the great Builder possessed his imagination. New ideas crowded upon him and drove his pencil at breakneck speed until he had covered several sheets; and when he stood up from the shadow of the rock and faced the glare of the sun, the sermon which had haunted him since his arrival at Billman was completed.

He glanced at the pages from time to time as he wandered back into the town; and before he reached his shack, he knew that the thing was firm in his memory. At his door he stood for a moment and watched the wind roll a cloud of dust up the street more swiftly than a horse could gallop. So let the idea which had come to him on this morning sweep through the minds of his auditors, and freshen in them the almost obliterated image of their Creator!

He entered his little house and was startled by the figure of a Dominican monk, whose fat body was covered with a gown of not overclean rusty black, girded with a long cord. The monk turned and grasped the hand of Ingram.

'Good morning, Mr. Ingram,' said he. 'I am Brother Pedrillo. I've come to welcome a fellow-worker to Billman.'

Ingram did not like the use of the word 'fellow-worker'. Young Mr. Ingram had been bred to a faith which does not look kindly upon the Roman Catholic creed; but in addition, he felt in himself so much aspiring vigor, such a contempt of the flesh, that to be yoked with Brother Pedrillo was like harnessing an ox in the same team with Pegasus.

So he turned away, busied himself putting up his notes for the sermon, and revolved swiftly in his mind the attitude which he should assume. However, the Lord works His will in mysterious ways. The Reverend Reginald decided that he would force himself into friendliness with the Dominican. Humility is ordained very early in the Gospel.

2

A Kindly Buzzard

He invited Brother Pedrillo to take a chair, and so became aware of the shoes of his visitor. They were made of roughest cowhide, but even that durable material was worn to tatters. The fringe of his robe, too, was worn to rags, and the bald head of the monk had been burned well-nigh black. At least this was a man who was much in the open air. The heart of young Ingram softened a little.

'You read philosophy, I see,' remarked the monk.

'Don't you?' queried Ingram, rather sharply.

'When I was just from school, yes,' replied the Dominican. 'But afterward, I let the thing slip. It was quite useless to me in my work.'

'Ah!' said Ingram coldly.

'Not,' added the other, 'that philosophy cannot be translated into the language and the acts of the man in the street; but I haven't the time nor the intelligence to do the translating. My work takes me long distances,' he explained more fully, 'and my tasks are placed far apart.' He pointed to his battered shoes.

'You don't live in Billman, then?' asked Ingram.

'I live in a district a hundred miles square.'

'Hello! Do you walk that?'

'Sometimes I get a lift in a buckboard. But my people are very poor. I must walk most of the days.'

'A frightful waste of time,' suggested Ingram.

'For those who live or for those who die,' said the Dominican, 'time is of little importance in this part of the world. Have you watched the buzzards?'

'Buzzards?'

'They wait on the wing a week at a time, without water, sailing a hundred leagues a day, perhaps; but, if they are watchful, finally they find food. It is that way with me. I go from village to village, from house to house. But if I find one good thing a month to do, I am satisfied. The rest of the time, I wait on the wing, as you might say.'

He looked down at his round stomach as he spoke, and laughed comfortably, until he shook from head to foot.

'I should think that you could settle down here,' said Ingram with enthusiasm. 'There are scores of Mexicans here. The number of their knife fights, you know – I beg your pardon,' he added, 'I don't want to appear to give advice.'

'Ah, but do it! Do it!' said Pedrillo. 'As we grow older we find little advice to take; and a great many occasions for giving. So say what is in your mind.'

Ingram looked at the other a little more closely, for he feared that he was being mocked; but he met an eye so transparent and a smile so genuine and childlike that he could not help laughing in return.

'There is nothing I can say,' he declared at last. 'Except that it seemed to me that there was enough in Billman to keep you busy every moment of your time.'

'In this little town,' said Pedrillo, 'my people shift so fast – up to the mines and back again, in and out – that I can do little except marry or bury them as they pass. If it were a settled place, then I could take a house here and live among them until I became really a brother to them. But as it is, the mines fill their pockets with money. They have plenty to spend on food and tequila, and something left over to gamble and fight for. Their minds and their hands are so filled that they have no need of me except when they are about to marry or to die. If I were to settle among them now they would forget that I am here. I would be a shadow to them. But since I come from a distance, at rare intervals, I am something more. They listen to me now and then. That is all I can expect. I am not ambitious, Mr. Ingram. But you have your own people, and they are not mine. All of mine will hear me – at least two or three times in their lives. Some of yours will never hear you at all. But a great many of them may take you into their everyday lives. That is the greater good. Unquestionably, the greater good. Ah, well, I must accept my destiny.'

His words were a good deal more serious than his manner, for he smiled as he spoke.

'But,' he added, 'I have never had gifts. Unless it is a gift to listen to people's sorrows. You, however, can mix with your kind and command admiration among them.'

'Why do you say that?' asked Ingram, frowning a little, as one who does not like to receive idle compliments.

'You are big,' said the Mexican; 'you are young, and you are strong. The men here are rough; but they cannot afford to scorn you.'

He pointed, as he spoke, to a little silver vase which stood on top of the bookshelf, a pair of boxing gloves chased on its side.

Young Ingram smiled faintly and shrugged his

shoulders.

'That was before I had any serious purpose in life,' said he. 'That was before I found myself. Now I'm a man.'

'How old are you?'

'Twenty-five, almost,' said Ingram.

Brother Pedrillo did not smile. 'And how did you come to find yourself?' he asked gently.

Ingram found it strangely easy to talk about himself to this brown, fat face, these inactive but knowing eyes. He rested his elbows on his knees and looked into the past.

'I was smashed in a football game, and played too long afterward. It put me in the hospital. I had the germs of a fever in me at the time, and that gave the sickness a galloping start. It was a long struggle. But in the intervals, when I was not delirious and when I realized how close to death I lay, I wondered what I had been doing with myself for twenty years. Twenty long years, and nothing done, nothing worth while! A few goals kicked. A few touchdowns. Some boxing. Well, I determined that if God spared me I would give something to the world that was worth while. And when I could call my life my own, I began studying for the church.'

He checked himself and looked rather suspiciously at the Brother.

'I seem to be chattering a good deal,' he

suggested.

'Talk is good,' said the older man with conviction. All at once he began to whistle a thin, small note. Ingram turned and saw a little yellow-backed lizard lying in the burning sun upon the threshold. It lifted its head and listened to the music. 'Talk is good,' added the friar, with a nod of surety.

He stood up.

'We begin to know each other,' he said.

'I want to ask you the same question that you asked me,' said Ingram. 'How did *you* happen to select your vocation?'

'But I had nothing to do with it,' answered the friar. 'My mother gave me to the church. And here I am,' he added, and smiled again. 'Whatever I can do, ask of me. I have little power. I have little knowledge. But I know something of the strong men who live here.'

'These ruffians!' cried Ingram rather fiercely.

Brother Pedrillo raised a brown hand.

'Don't call them that. Yes, call them that if you will. It is always better to put it into words than to leave it buried in the mind. But except for a rough man's act, would there be a church here now? Would you yourself be here in the desert, my brother?'

Ingram bit his lip thoughtfully.

'I don't know what you mean,' he replied

frankly.

'You don't know?' asked Pedrillo, his smile fading. And for a single instant his eyes were keen and cold as they searched the face of his companion. 'Perhaps you don't,' he decided. 'You have not heard how your own church was built?'

'By a man named William Luger. I've been here only four days, you understand.'

'Do you not know how he came to leave the money for it?'

'No. Not yet.'

'So, so!' murmured the friar.

He sat down again and rolled a cigarette, whistling the small note to the enchanted lizard at the door. He made the cigarette like a little cornucopia, for such is the Mexican fashion. And Ingram saw, with a little disgust, that the fingers of the holy man were literally painted orange-yellow by the stain of nicotine.

'Let me tell you,' said the friar, beginning to blow smoke toward the rough beams of the ceiling. 'Billy Luger was a man typical of this part of the world.'

'A little better than that, I hope,' said Ingram, turning stiff.

'No,' replied the Dominican. 'He was just that. He had spent thirty years branding cattle – his own or ones he borrowed for the occasion. Finally he dipped into mining, when the rush started toward the San Joaquin silver and the Sierra Negra gold. He made a few thousand and was celebrating a trip to town one evening, when he got into a card game with 'Red Jim' Moffet. Moffet shot him, and it was while Billy lay dying that he made up his mind to leave his money for the founding of a church. That's the story. And that's what brought you here.'

'And the murderer?' asked Mr. Ingram hotly. 'He was hanged, I trust?'

'You are a sanguinary young man,' smiled the Dominican. 'But these people are fond of killing with guns; they rarely kill with a rope. No, Moffet was not hanged. He's still alive, prosperous and well. You'll meet him around the town.'

'A most extraordinary tale,' said Ingram, breathing hard. 'Was no attempt made to bring his killer to justice?'

'The fact is,' said the friar sympathetically, 'that Moffet accused Billy of having a card up his sleeve during the game. And I believe that the bystanders agreed with Red, after the smoke blew away.'

Brother Pedrillo rose again.

'You are going to exercise much influence from the start, I know,' said he.

'And on what do you base that?' asked Ingram, again antagonistic.

'Where the ladies of the town go, the men are

sure to follow – though sometimes at a little distance,' said Pedrillo, and he stepped out into the blast of the sun.

It glistened on his bald head as upon brown glass.

Once more the friar waved adieu, and trudged down the dusty street, leaving Ingram of two minds as he stood in the doorway. He could not quite make out the import of that last remark. It sounded suspiciously like a touch of sarcasm, but he could not be sure. At length he turned to complete his sermon. It was not easy. He had to set his teeth and force his pencil on. Because from time to time across his mind came the vision of a card game – and one man with cards up the sleeve!

3

With Tears in Her Eyes

Women? He had not guessed that there were so many in the entire town, aside from the Mexican section across the creek. They filled more than half the front part of the church, whispering, buzzing, and then settling down to watch his face with a curious insistence, until he began to feel that they were hearing not a word.

He lifted his eyes from them and directed the strength of his little oration toward a dozen men who remained as far back as possible on the benches, huddling themselves into the shadowy corners.

They were listening, and they did not seem convinced by this talk about peace. Now and then they looked gravely at one another. Once or twice the Reverend Reginald Ingram thought he saw a faint smile. But he could not be sure. Only he knew that the church now began to seem extremely small; and that the sun beat upon it with a terrific force. It was hot, very hot; and he wanted a cooling wind to pour in and bring him relief.

Well, that small miracle was denied for his gratification, and Ingram centered his attention fiercely on his sermon – bulldogging it through, as he often had done on the football field. Yardage on a football field, however, is chalked off with convenient white lines. Yardage in a church is a different matter. One may be under the goal posts one instant, and fighting to keep from being scored on the next.

However, he drew his parallels. The yellow beetle and the gay little wren were called upon to furnish a metaphor apiece. The cruel hawk was not mentioned at all. And gradually he established his own conviction in the picture he was drawing of peace on earth, and good will among all of the men living upon it. He felt that he was drawing his audience together a little more. As for the hulking men in the rear – let them rise and sidle with creaking boots toward the exit. Not one of the feminine heads before him turned to watch them go. No, all were feverishly concentrated upon him. They were brown faces, indubitably

Anglo-Saxon in spite of their color. And the eyes seemed strangely blue and bright by contrast. He began to feel that never before had he seen so many intelligent women gathered together. For, if the truth must be known, Mr. Ingram looked down upon the other sex. They rarely bothered him. No woman can talk football, and few can talk of religion with much conviction.

The minister ended his sermon, and the organ responded in squawks of protest to the organist who was trying to furnish music to close the service. However, the little crowd did not depart, and Ingram, descending from his throne, was softly enveloped in a wave of organdies and lawns that brought a fresh, wholesome laundry smell about him.

The ladies introduced themselves, and he listened gravely and earnestly to their names. If he was to work with such material as this, then it behooved him, by all means, to come quickly to the knowledge of it.

They had enjoyed his sermon, it appeared. They had enjoyed it, oh, so much! Everything he said was *so* true. If one only stopped to think! How well he understood the desert, and their problems! Some one was asking him to come home to lunch. And then another, and another.

A girl with very pale, blonde hair and very blue, blue eyes seemed to brush all the others aside, with her gesture – though she was a little thing – and stood directly before him, smiling up.

'They have no right to you,' said she. 'My poor mother couldn't come, and she wanted me to remember every word you said. As if I could do that, in my silly head! So you have to come home to lunch with me. Go away, Charlotte! Don't be foolish! Of course Mr. Ingram is coming with me!'

Even among the others it seemed to be taken for granted that Mr. Ingram would, of course, go with her of the pale hair and the extraordinarily blue eyes. They gave up. And she carried him off from the church.

Indeed, he had a distinct impression that he was being carried. He could remember her name by a little effort; in fact, it was a very odd one. She was called Astrid Vasa.

As they came from the church a tall man, who looked compressed by his store clothes and nearly strangled by his necktie, approached them, with a red-faced grin for the girl.

'Come along, Red,' said she. 'This is Red Moffet, Mr. Ingram. Red, this is Mr. Ingram. You know. He runs the church, and everything. Don't you, Mr. Ingram?'

She looked up at Mr. Ingram at the conclusion of this infantile question, and shut out the view of Red Moffet with a parasol which slanted over one shoulder, and which she was spinning with a very delicately made little hand. Ingram wanted to frown, but he couldn't help smiling; which made him more determined than ever to frown. And so his smile grew broad!

'Red works in a mine, or something,' explained Astrid Vasa, shrugging a shoulder in the direction of Mr. Moffet.

'I *own* a mine,' said Red. 'It's kind of different.'

He was offended, of course. It occurred vaguely to Ingram that Mr. Moffet seemed *very* offended. For his own part, he wondered what his attitude should be toward the man who had killed the founder of the church over which he now presided. But after all, it was said that the other cheek must be turned. Ingram, concentrating on the thought, set his teeth.

They reached a picket fence in front of a little unpainted house. Few of the houses in Billman were painted, for that matter. 'I dunno that I'll be comin' in,' said Red Moffet gloomily.

'You better come along,' said Astrid. 'We gotta couple of the best-looking roosters that you ever saw for dinner.'

'I'm kind of busy,' said Red, more darkly than ever. 'So long!'

And he rambled down the street with a peculiarly awkward leg action. It reminded

Ingram of the stride of a certain tackle of his college team, a fellow uncannily skillful in getting down the field under a kick, and marvelous in providing interference. He was more interested in Red Moffet from that instant.

'He's got a grouch on,' confided Astrid. 'He always wants to be the whole show since he got his silly old mine. C'mon in!'

The screen door screeched as it was kicked open from within. A burly gentleman in shirt sleeves stood before them.

'Hello; where's Red?' asked he in a pleasant voice.

'Dad, this is Mr. Ingram, the minister, and he's just been persuaded to –'

'Hullo, Ingram! Glad see you. Where's Red, sis?'

'I dunno. He got a grouch on and beat it. I can't be bothered – all his notions.'

'You little simp,' said the inelegant Mr. Vasa, 'you'll be havin' him slide through your fingers one of these days.'

'Dad, what *are* you talkin' about?' exclaimed Astrid, very pink.

Her sire looked from her to her companion and grunted.

'Humph,' said he. 'Is that it, eh?'

'Is that what?' asked Astrid, furious.

'Aw, nothin'. C'min and sit down and rest your

feet, Ingram. Lookit – ain't it like a fool girl, though? Shufflin' a boy like Red around? Know Red, I guess?'

'I've barely met him,' said Ingram, with reserve.

'Have, eh? Well, he's all right. Kind of mean, sometimes. Yep, mean as hell. But straight. Awful straight. Why, that kid's got a half million dollars' worth of mine up in the San Joaquin. Wouldn't think it, would you, to look at him? But I've seen it. Make your mouth water. Lord knows how deep the vein runs. Maybe take out a hundred thousand a year for a hundred years. Can't tell. And here's our Astie with a gent like that in her pocket, and chucking him away over her shoulder. Finders keepers! Sis, you're a simp. That's all!'

'Father!' cried Astrid, dividing the word into two distinct parts, each concealing a world of meaning. 'D'you know that you're talkin' to a minister, with all your profanity, and – and talking foolishness about Red Moffet? Who said I had him in my pocket? Who wants to have him there? I'm sure I don't. And – what do you *mean* by talking like this to a perfect stranger?'

'Aw, don't step on your own toes to spite me, sis,' suggested her father, grinning. 'Besides, maybe Ingram ain't going to be a stranger for very long. How about it?'

This extreme directness embarrassed Ingram.

He searched his mind – and found nothing with which to respond except a smile which might have received varying interpretations. Astrid retreated to regain her composure and let her blushes settle down to a normal pink.

'She's a good kid,' pronounced Mr. Vasa, 'but careless. Dog-gone careless. Far as that goes, though, this here is a land of carelessness and accidents. Billman's an accident, you know.'

'An accident?' said the polite Ingram.

'Sure. You know how it started?'

'No. Started?'

'Sure. A town has to start, don't it? Aw, you're fresh out of the old States, where a town put down roots so long ago that there ain't any story left about it except a legend that's a lie. Well, things ain't that way out here. We ain't scratched many wrinkles on the desert yet, and the only ones we've made are all new. Take Billman. Old Ike Billman was started for the San Joaquin range when the mines opened up there. Had a string of wagons loaded with stuff to sell for ten prices, the old hound! But he busted down here. Broke a wagon wheel. Before he got it fixed the boys were rushing through on the way for the San Joaquin on one side and for the Sierra Negra on the other. They wanted supplies, and wanted 'em so bad that price was no object. So Ike, he piled out his stuff and sold it out here just as good as he could have done if he'd marched all the way into the mountains. Then he put up a shack, and began freighting more stuff – not to the mines, but here. Other folks followed the good example. Then some of us have got interests in both places – San Joaquin and Sierra Negra – so we live in this halfway station. Y'understand? That's how Billman started growing. Just plain accident.'

'You're a mine owner also, then?' said Ingram in a polite attempt to discover the interests of his host.

Astrid returned. She had studied her smile before the mirror and felt that it would do.

'Sure, I'm a mine owner. I mean, I got shares in a couple of mines. I was a blacksmith when I come out here to –'

'Dad,' put in Astrid, 'I don't see why you have to rake up all the old family history. I'm sure Mr. Ingram isn't interested.'

'Why not?' asked Vasa. 'Ain't it honest to be a blacksmith? I never was in jail – except overnight. I got nothing to be ashamed of. It's a darn good trade, Ingram – blacksmithing. The money that I made out of it was honest. But this mining game – just luck! I took a couple of flyers at it. And they both connected with the bull's-eye. There you are. I'm gunna be pretty well off. I could sell out now for a hundred thousand. Maybe more. Not so bad, eh? But I guess I was just as happy hammering iron, hot or cold. It's the thing that you're cut out for that counts. Luck ain't apt to make you happy, Ingram. I'll never be worth shucks as a miner. But I could lay a shoe on the hoof of a horse so fine it would make you stare. You come and watch me some day. I still put in a few hours in the old shop now and then, just to keep my hand in.'

Mrs. Vasa, as small as her husband was large, rather withered but still good looking, stood in the doorway. She was flushed from her work in the kitchen, and wiped her hands on her apron before she greeted the minister.

'Astie says that the sermon was just wonderful. I'll bet it was,' said Mrs. Vasa. 'Now you come along in and have a bite of lunch with us, will you? I'm mighty glad to have you here, Mr. Ingram. I was just too busy to get to church this morning. Church is kind of new in Billman, you know. And it takes a body a time to get into the run of going again. But my folks were mighty regular; they never missed a Sunday hardly. I always think it does you sort of good to go to church. Cools you off, you know, and it's restful. D'you think that you're gunna like Billman, Mr. Ingram?'

This was poured out effortlessly, rapidly, as they got to the table and sat down. Mr. Ingram could have made a quick answer to the final question, but it was not necessary to answer questions in this house. Between the head of the house and his wife there was no room left for silent spots.

Afterward they had music. Ingram sat down to supper, and remained to listen in amazement.

'Astie, she sings like a bird; doggone me if she don't!' said her father.

And that was exactly what she did. She accompanied herself on the piano. As smoothly as speech flowed from the lips of Mrs. Vasa, so song poured from the throat of her daughter, and the accompaniment bubbled delightfully in between.

'Dragged that dog-gone piano clean out from Comanche Crossing,' declared Vasa. 'And I never regretted what it cost, derned if I have. Now ain't it a treat to have a girl that can sing like that? She ought to be on the stage, where thousands could enjoy her. Honest, she should. But she'll never get there.'

'Why do you say that, dad?' asked Mrs. Vasa.

'Because she's got her career all mapped and laid out for her right here in Billman,' said the head of the house.

'Career?' asked Astrid. 'What sort of career?'

'Humph!' said the ex-blacksmith. 'Breakin' hearts, or tryin' to!'

'Dad, you're just –' cried Astrid.

'You might let the poor girl –' began Mrs. Vasa.

'Aw, be still!' said Vasa. 'Ingram's gunna know about you pretty quick, if he don't already. I tell you what, Ingram. If that girl hadn't been born with a pretty face, she would have amounted to something. But she's got just enough good looks to spoil her. Her heart's all right. But her mirror keeps tellin' her that she's Cleopatra.'

'I hope you don't pay no attention, the way that he keeps on about his own flesh and blood,' said Mrs. Vasa to her guest.

Ingram smiled. But it was with an effort.

'Tune up, sis,' commanded Vasa. 'Go on and tune up, will you, and stop shaking your head at me. It ain't gunna change me. I'm too old to change. Take me or leave me. That's my motto. Maybe there's rough hammer marks on me, but the stuff I'm made of is the right iron, I think. Go on and sing, will you? Gimme some of the old ones, where you don't have to listen too hard. "Annie Laurie", that's about my speed. Somethin' nice and sad. Or "Ben Bolt". Dog-gone me, if that ain't a swell song, Mr. Ingram. What you say? "Ben Bolt", sis. And make her nice and sobby!'

They had 'Ben Bolt' and 'Annie Laurie,' also.

And afterward Mr. Vasa went to sleep in his chair and snored. And Mrs. Vasa announced that she would go and close her eyes for a minute. Such a warm afternoon! Mr. Ingram was glad to excuse her. He sat in the shade of the house with Astrid.

'I guess you think we're terrible people,' said Astrid sadly, 'the way that dad carries on.'

'No,' said Ingram earnestly. 'I don't think so at all. I like him. He doesn't pretend. He's honest. I like him a great deal, you know.'

It was pleasant to see her face light. Her smile was like her singing, charming beyond words. And Ingram wondered how such a flower could have grown in such rocky soil. It made him feel, too, the value of that background of culture which enables one to appreciate the great and the simple, the complex and the homely.

'He thinks I ought to go on the stage,' said Astrid. 'But I'll never get there. No, I'll have to stay here in the desert.'

'Do you want to go?'

'I don't know,' said she. 'Only – I'm so lonely here.'

She looked up at him with sad eyes.

'Poor child!' said Ingram, melting. 'Lonely?'

He leaned a little toward her. Charitable kindness is commanded directly.

'Oh, lonely, lonely!' sighed Astrid, still looking into his face with suffering eyes. 'Do you know – but you wouldn't want me to tell you –'

'I think I would,' said the gentle minister.

'You know such a lot, and you're so wise and clever,' said Astrid, 'you would laugh at me!'

'I'm none of those things. And I won't laugh.'

'Really you won't?'

'No.'

'Well, of course I know a lot of people here. But though there are lots of them to chatter to – well, perhaps you won't understand – there's really not a soul for me to talk to.'

'Poor child!' said Mr. Ingram. He felt that he had said that before, but it was so true that he could not help repeating it. 'Poor child, of course I can understand!'

'Until you came, Mr. Ingram. And I really think that I could talk to you.'

'You shall, my dear. Of course you shall, whenever you please.'

'And you won't laugh at me?'

'Certainly not.'

'And when I tire you, you'll just send me away?'

'We'll see about that,' said he, tolerantly.

'Ah, you could understand!' said Astrid. 'The others – they just think that I'm always gay. They never guess, Mr. Ingram, how close – the tears are – sometimes!'

Yes, yes! But he could guess! He could see the tears now, just welling into her eyes. And he dropped a large, strong hand over her little one.

They sat in silence. He felt prepared to face the world. He felt the ability to endure, to suffer. And some day, when he had children, he was sure that he would be able to raise them tenderly, and well.

4

Around the Corner from Nowhere

There followed for Ingram several days of severe labor, for he was establishing his parish, enlisting the interests of various people, and accepting sundry contributions which poured in with amazing speed for the first public work which he attempted. This was the establishment of a little hospital.

Sick men came down constantly from the mines in the San Joaquin, or in the Sierra Negra, and from Billman they were in the habit of taking the long stage journey overland to Comanche Crossing, where they could get medical attention of a kind. Ingram saw the possibility of putting up something which would be more than a way-station for the sick. And his idea was taken up enthusiastically. Mexican labor made the adobe bricks rapidly on the banks of the creek, and the terrible sun dried them to the proper strength; after that, skilled Mexican workers raised the walls of the hospital. There were three main rooms, and they were built of generous size, with lofty ceilings and thick walls, so that the sun's heat would not turn the place into an oven. For bed equipment there were various improvisations, and many donations were made after Ingram set the example by giving up his own cot. If he were willing to sleep on the floor, others would be equally brave in facing uncomfortable nights on the boards. For doctors there was no want; for several of them were among the men who had tried their luck in the gold rush and had run out of funds. They returned to their professional work and supplied the hospital with a competent staff. The Mexicans made excellent nurses, assisted from time to time by volunteers from among the ladies of Ingram's congregation. As for the funds to pay for all this necessary labor and expenses of various kinds, the inhabitants of Billman willingly dug deep into their purses, and in addition came contributions from all the mines.

The work of the hospital filled Ingram's hands for some time, and won for him a great deal of friendly recognition. In the meantime, a building of another kind went on to completion; a sure sign that the old days of Billman were drawing to a close, and that civilization was gathering the wild little town into its arms. For one day a thin, small man came to Ingram, a being so withered and lean that he seemed like a special product of the desert environment, equipped by nature to live for a long time without moisture of any kind. His skinny neck projected from a collar that would have girt in comfort the throat of a giant. His footwear was not neat. And when he fixed his melancholy eyes upon the minister, the latter was sure that this was another one of the race of hobos who pestered him from time to time.

Said the little man: 'I'm Sheriff Ted Connors. I came over to fix up a jail in this town, because it looks to me like this would be a handy place for a jail to stand. It wouldn't never have to be empty. And I'd like to know from you, how you get the folks in this town to fork over the money for a good cause?'

The two spent a long hour going over ways and means. And the very next day the foundations of the jail were established by the running of a shallow trench through the surface sands. The jail was completed in a very few days. And the withered little sheriff jogged out of town, leaving his work to be carried on by a younger, bigger, and much more formidable-looking deputy, Dick

Binney.

'Now that there's a church and a jail,' said big Vasa, 'it looks like Billman was pretty well collared, eh?'

Ingram agreed. It was, he felt, only a matter of waiting a few weeks for the lawlessness and roughness of the town to subside. He had had a taste of that lawlessness before the town was very old. For, one night – the hospital had been opened that day and the first patients, the wrecked victims of a mine explosion, installed – masked men entered Ingram's shack and bade him come with them.

They led him down the main street, which was singularly deserted, and out from the town to a point where a crowd was gathered under one of the few trees of the neighborhood. Beneath that tree stood a man whose hands were tied behind him; around his neck was the noose of a rope which had been flung over a limb above his head. Ingram realized that he was in the presence of a crew of vigilantes.

A gruff voice said to him: 'Here's Chuck Lane, that wants to talk to you, kid, before he swings. Hop to it and finish the job pronto. We're sleepy!'

'Do you intend to hang this man,' asked Ingram, 'without the process of law?'

'Ah!' said the leader of the crowd, 'is that your line? Now look here, kid, if there's gunna be any arguin' about that out of you, you can turn around and go home. Chuck swiped a horse, the skunk, and he's gunna swing for it. There's been too much borrowin' of horses around these parts lately. And he goes up as example number one. If you got any talkin' to do, do it on Chuck, will you?'

Ingram considered briefly. After all, he was quite helpless before these armed fellows. A protest would accomplish no good; it would merely deprive the victim of whatever spiritual comfort he might desire.

As he stepped up to the man who wore the noose, the others, with an unexpected sense of decency, made a wider circle around them.

'It's all right, boys,' said Chuck Lane cheerfully, noticing this backward movement. 'All I got to say can be heard by you gents.'

'Chuck,' said the minister, 'are you guilty of the crime of which they accuse you?'

'Crime?' echoed Chuck. 'If borrowin' a horse when a man's in a hurry is a crime – sure, I'm guilty! Well, kid, that ain't why they sent for you. Fact is, I want to know something from you.'

'Very well,' said Ingram, 'if you are a member of any church –'

'I was took to church once when I was a kid,' said the thief. 'Otherwise I ain't been bothered about them. But now when I come to stand here, around the corner from Nowhere, it seems to me a pretty good time to find out what's on the other side. What do you say, Ingram?'

'Do you mean that you have doubts?' asked Ingram.

'Sure! Doubts about everything. Is this the finish – like going to sleep and never waking up? You're a smart young feller. No matter what lingo you're paid to sling in the church, you give me the low-down out here, man to man. I won't tell nobody what you've said.'

'There is a life to come, surely,' said Ingram.

'Will you gimme a proof, then?'

'Yes. The beasts have flesh and sense. Man has something more. He is born with flesh, mind, and spirit. Mind and flesh die, but the spirit is imperishable.'

'You say it pretty slick and sure,' remarked Chuck Lane. 'You really mean that?'

'Yes.'

'Well, then, the next thing is: What chance have I to slip through without – without –'

'What chance have you of happiness?' asked the minister gently. 'That I cannot tell. You know your own mind and life.'

'What difference does the life make, really?' asked the horse thief. 'Ain't it what's in the head that counts most?'

'Yes,' said Ingram. 'Sin is more in the mind than in the body. Have you anything on your conscience?'

'Me? Well, not much. I've taken my fun where I've found it, as somebody has said before me. I knifed a gent in Chihuahua, once. But that was a fair fight. He'd taken a pass at me with a chair. I shot a fellow up in Butte, too. But the hound had told everybody that he was going to get me. So that don't count, either. Otherwise, there ain't been nothing important. This little job about the horse – that's nothing. I was just in a hurry. Now, kid, the cards are on the table. Where do I go?'

'You are young,' said Ingram. 'You're not much more than thirty –'

'I'm twenty-two.'

The minister stared, aghast. Much, much of life had been scored on the face of this young man in his few short years.

Chuck seemed to understand, for he went on: 'But the wrinkles don't set till you're forty,' he remarked, 'and you can change your face up to that time. Y'understand?'

'Did you intend to take up some other way of –'

'I was always aiming to be a farmer, if I could get a stake together. Nothin' wrong with my intentions, but the money was lackin'.'

'And how did you try to earn it?'

'Cards was my chief line.'

'Gambling?'

'Yes.'

'You were honest, Chuck?'

'I never had the fingers for real crookedness,' admitted Chuck frankly. 'I could palm a couple of cards. That was all. And I generally met up with somebody a good deal slicker than I was. So my winnings went out the window.'

Ingram was silent.

'Does that make it bad for me?' asked Chuck ingenuously.

It was a grim moment in which to play the judge, but Ingram answered slowly: 'You've been a man-killer, a thief, and a crooked gambler. And perhaps there have been other things.'

'Well,' said Chuck, 'I suppose that closes the door on me?'

'I don't know,' said Ingram. 'It depends, in the first place, upon your repentance.'

'Repentance?' echoed the other. 'Well, I dunno that I feel bad about th' way I've lived. I've never shot a man in the back, and I've never cheated a drunk or a fool at the cards. I tried to trim the sharks, and the sharks always trimmed me.'

'Is that all?' said Ingram.

'That's about all. Except that I'd sure like to get with the right crowd of boys on the other side. I never had no real use for the tinhorns, thugs, and short sports that must be crowded into hell, Ingram. But you think I got a mighty slim chance, eh?'

Wistfulness and manly courage struggled in his voice.

'No man can judge you,' said the young minister. 'If you believe in the goodness of God, and fix your mind on that belief, you may be saved, Chuck. I shall pray for you.'

'Do it, old-timer,' said Chuck. 'A prayer or two wouldn't do me any harm, and it might do me a lot of good. And – look here – hey, boys!'

'Well?' asked some one, coming closer.

'I'd like Ingram to have my guns. It's all that I've got to leave the world.'

'Are there no messages that I can take for you?' asked Ingram.

'I don't want to think about the folks that I leave behind me,' said the thief. 'I got a girl down in – well, let it go. It's better for her never to hear than it is for her to start grievin' about me. Better to think that I run off and forgot to come back to her. So long, Ingram!'

'Gentlemen,' said Ingram, turning on the crowd, 'I protest against this unwarranted –'

'Rustle the kid out of the way,' said some one, and half a dozen strong pairs of hands hurried Chuck suddenly away.

Behind him Ingram heard a groan, as of strong friction, and, glancing back, saw something swinging pendulous beneath the tree, and writhing against the golden surface of the rising moon.

5

A Gent With a Gun

The death of Chuck Lane caused a good deal of excitement in the town, for he was no common or ordinary thief, and the minister overheard one most serious conversation the next day.

He had stopped at Vasa's house to talk over the choir work with pretty Astrid; for she led the choir for him, and a thorough good job she made of it. There he met Red Moffet, and Red, with an ugly glance, rose and strode away, barely grunting at the minister as he passed.

'I think Red doesn't like me very well,' said Ingram. 'He seems to have something against me. Do you guess what it is?'

'I can't guess,' said Astrid, with the strangest of smiles. 'I haven't the least idea!'

But now the gallant form of the deputy sheriff,

Dick Binney, swept down the street, and Red Moffet hailed him suddenly and strongly from the sidewalk.

'Binney! Hey, Binney!'

The deputy sheriff reined in his horse. The dust cloud he had raised blew down the street, and left him with the shimmering heat of the sun drenching him. So terrible was the brightness of that light, and so great the radiation of heat from every surface, that sometimes it seemed to the young minister that he lived in a ghost world here on the edge of the desert. All was unreal, surrounded by airy lines of imagination, or radiating heat.

Unreal now were those two men, and the horse which one of them bestrode. But very real was the voice of Red Moffet, calling: 'Binney, were you there last night?'

'Was I where?'

'You know where.'

'I dunno what you mean.'

'Was you one of them that hung up poor Chuck Lane?'

'Me? The sheriff of this here place? What you take me for, anyway? Are you crazy?'

'I dunno what I take you for. But I've heard a yarn that you was with the rest of them cowards and sneaks that killed poor Chuck.'

Dick Binney dismounted suddenly from his horse.

'I dunno how to take this here,' said he. 'I dunno whether it's aimed at the boys who hanged Chuck last night, or at me!'

'I say,' declared Moffet, 'that Chuck was an honester man than any of them that strung him up. And if you was one of them, that goes for you, too!'

It seemed that the deputy was willing enough to take offense, but he paused and gritted his teeth, between passion and caution. Certainly it would not do for him to avow that he had been one of the masked men.

So he said: 'What you say don't bother me, Red. But if you're out and lookin' for trouble, I'm your man, all right!'

'Bah!' sneered Red Moffet. 'It wouldn't please you none to make trouble for any man in town, now that you got the law behind you! You can do your killings with a posse now.'

'Can I?' replied Binney, equally furious. 'I would never need a posse to account for you, young feller!'

'Is that a promise, Binney?' asked Moffet. 'Are you askin' me to have a meetin' with you one day?'

'Whenever you like,' said the deputy. 'But now *I'm* busy. I ain't gunna stand here and waste time with a professional gun fighter like you, Moffet. Only, I give you a warning. You got to watch yourself around this part of the world from now on. I'm watchin' you. I'm gunna give you just enough rope to hang yourself.'

He jumped back into the saddle, and galloped down the street, leaving Red Moffet shaking a fist after him and cursing volubly.

Mr. Vasa, coming home, paused to listen with a judicious air to the linguistic display of Red. Then he came into his yard, shaking his head gravely.

'I'll tell you what it is,' said Vasa, greeting his daughter and the minister, 'things ain't what they used to be around these parts. There's a terrible fallin' off of manhood all around! There's a terrible fallin' off! There's been enough language used up by Red and Dick Binney, yonder, to have got a whole town shot up in the palmy days that I could tell you about.'

'Dad!' cried his daughter.

'Look here,' said the ex-blacksmith, 'don't you make a profession of being shocked every time I open my mouth. You live and learn, honey! I tell you, there was never no fireworks in the way of words shot off before the boys reached for their guns in the old days, Ingram. No, sir! I remember when I was standing in the old Parker saloon. That was a cool place. Always wet down the floor every hour and sprinkled fresh, wet sawdust around. Made a drink taste a lot better. It was like spring inside that place, no matter how much summer there might be in the street. Well, young

Mitchell was in there, drinking. Same fellow that shot Pete Brewer in the back. He was drinkin' and yarnin' about a freighting job that he'd come in from. He ordered up a round.

' "I'll buy one for the boys," says he.

' "No, you won't," says a voice.

'We looked across, and there was Tim Lafferty that had just come through the swingin' doors.

' "Why won't I?" asks Mitchell.

' "You ain't got time!" says Tim.

'They went for their guns right then, and as I stepped back out of line two bullets crossed in front of my face. Neither of 'em missed. But it was Mitchell that died. Well, that was about as much conversation as they needed in the old days before they had a fight. But now, look at the way that those two have been wastin' language in the street; and nothing done about it. I say, it's disgusting!'

'Do you think that Red's a coward?' asked the girl sharply.

'Red? Naw! He ain't a coward. And he can shoot. But what's important is that the fashion has changed now. A gent with a gun that he wants to use feels that he's got to write a book about his intentions before he can burn any powder. They didn't waste themselves on introductions in the old days. Well, those times will never come back.'

The minister asked gravely: 'Is it possible that

the deputy sheriff could have been at the lynching the other night?'

'Well, and why not?'

'Why not? The representative of the law –'

'Why, old Connors made a terrible mistake when he up and appointed Dick for the job. Dick is all right some ways. But he's got an idea that the law is to be more useful to him than to the rest of the folks. He hated Chuck. I got an idea that he *was* at the hanging. And that's why Red is mad. He loved Chuck. Good boy, that Chuck Lane.'

'Did you know him?' asked the minister, with some eagerness.

'Did I know myself? Sure, I knew him!'

'He was a gambler and – a horse thief?'

'That was careless – swiping the horse. Matter of fact, though, if he'd got to the other end of the line, he would have sent back the coin to pay for the horse as soon as he got enough money together. But you got to judge people according to their own lights, and not according to yours, young man!'

Thus spoke Mr. Vasa, with the large assurance of one who has lived in this world and knows a good deal about it.

'It's a brutal thing to lynch any man, no matter how guilty,' declared Ingram.

'Hey, hold on!' cried the blacksmith. 'Matter of fact, there ain't enough organized law around here to shake a stick at. Not half enough! And I don't blame the boys that hung up Chuck. Can't let horse stealing go on!'

This double sympathy on the part of Mr. Vasa amazed and silenced Ingram.

'You're lookin' thin,' went on Vasa. 'Tell me how you're likin' the town. You run along into the house, Astie, will you? I got to talk to Ingram.'

Astrid rose, smiled at her guest, and went slowly toward the house.

'She's got a sweet smile, ain't she?' was the rather abrupt beginning of the blacksmith's speech.

'She has,' said Ingram thoughtfully. 'Yes,' he added, as though turning the matter in his mind and agreeing thoroughly, 'yes, she has a lovely smile. She– she's a fine girl, I think.'

'Pretty little kid,' declared the father, yawning. 'But she ain't so fine. No, not so fine as you'd think. Wouldn't do a lick of housework. I don't think, if her life depended on it. Y'understand?'

'Ah?' said Ingram, vaguely offended by this familiarity.

'And she's fond of everything that money can be spent on. Look at that pony of hers. Took her down to look over a whole herd at the McCormick sale. Nothin' would do for her. "I'll take that little brown horse, dad," says she.

' "Now, Astie," says I, "don't you be a little fool.

That little brown horse is a racer, out of blood more ancienter than the dog-gone kings of England. For a fact!"

' "All right," says she, and turns her shoulder.

' "Look yonder at that fine chestnut," says I. "There's a fine, gentle, upstanding horse. Half-bred. Strong, not a flaw in it anywhere. Warranted good disposition. Mouth like silk. Footwork on the mountains like a mule. Go like a camel without water. Now, Astie, how would you like it for me to give you that fine horse – and ain't he a beauty, too?"

' "I don't want it," says she. "It'll do for that cross-eyed Mame Lucas, maybe!"

' "Astie," says I, "what would you do with a horse that would buck you over its head the minute that you got into the saddle?"

' "Climb into the saddle again," says she.

' "Bah!" says I.

' "Bah yourself!" says she.

'It made me mad, and I bought that dog-gone brown horse. Guess for what? Eleven hundred iron men! Yes, sir!

' "Now, you ride him home!" says I, hoping that he'd break her neck.

'He done his best, but she's made of India rubber. Threw her five times on the way, and had half the town chasing the horse for her. But she rode him all the way home, and then went to bed for three days. But now he eats out of her hand. Wouldn't think that she had that much spunk, would you?'

'No,' agreed the minister, amazed. 'I would not!'

'Nobody would,' said the blacksmith, 'to look at the sappy light in her eyes a good deal of the time. But I'm tellin' you true. Expensive! That's what that kid is. If there was ten pairs of shoes in a store window, she'd pick out the most high-priced pair blindfold. She's got an instinct for it, I tell you!'

Ingram smiled.

'You think that she'd change, maybe,' said the blacksmith. 'But she won't. It's bred in the bone. God knows where she got it, though. Her ma was never an expensive woman.'

He rolled a cigarette with a single twist of his powerful fingers, and scratched a match on the thigh of his trousers. A hundred more or less faint lines showed where other matches had been lighted on the same cloth.

'This ain't a blind trail that I been followin',' he announced. 'I'm leadin' up to something. D'you guess what?'

'No,' said Ingram. 'I really don't guess what you may have in mind.'

'I thought you wouldn't,' said Vasa. 'Some of you smart fellows couldn't cut for sign with a five-year-old half-wit. Matter of fact, what I want to know is: Where are you heading with sis?'

'Heading with her?' said Ingram, very blank.

'Where d'you drift? What's your name with her? Does she call you deary, yet?'

Mr. Ingram stared.

'Has she held your hand yet for you?' asked Vasa.

The blood of a line of ancient ancestors curdled in the veins of Mr. Ingram.

'She does all of those things to the boys,' said the blacksmith. 'There is even two or three that may have kissed her. I dunno. But not many. She gets a little soft and soapy. But she's all right; I'd trust Astie in the crowd. I wondered where you'd been sizin' up with her?'

'I don't know what you mean,' declared the minister.

'Aw, come on!' grinned the other, very amiably. 'Everybody has to love Astie. Some love her a little. Some love her a lot. Even the girls can't hate her. How d'you stand? Love her a little? Love her a lot?'

Ingram began to turn pink. Partly with embarrassment, and partly with anger.

'I have for Astrid,' he said with deliberation, 'a brotherly regard –'

'Hell!' said Vasa.

The word exploded from his thick lips.

'What kind of drivel is this?' he demanded.

At this, Ingram narrowed his eyes a little and sat a bit forward. More than one football stalwart who had seen that expression in the eyes of Ingram had winced in the old days. But the blacksmith endured this gaze with the calm of one who carries a gun and knows how to use it. Who carries two hundred and thirty pounds of muscle, also – and knows how to use it!

'Don't give me the chilly eye like that, kid,' he continued. 'I aim to find out where you stand with Astie. Will you talk?'

'Your daughter,' said the minister, 'is a very pleasant girl, and I presume that that closes this part of the conversation?'

He stood up. The blacksmith rose also.

'Well,' said Vasa, glowering, 'suppose we shake hands and part friends on it?'

'Certainly,' said Ingram.

A vast, rather grimy paw closed over his hand, and suddenly he felt a pressure like the force of a powerful clamp, grinding the metacarpal bones together. But pulling a good oar on a powerful eight does not leave one with the grip of a child. The leaner, bonier fingers of Ingram curled into the plump grip of Vasa, secured a purchase, and began to gather strength.

Suddenly Vasa cursed and tore his hand away.

'Sit down again,' he said suddenly, looking at his splotchy hand. 'Sit down again. I didn't think you was as much of a man as this! It's what comes of layin' off work. I'm soft!'

The minister, breathing rather hard, sat down as invited. He waited, silently.

'You see, Ingram,' said the blacksmith, 'I've watched sis with the other boys, and I've watched her with you. She's always been getting a bit dizzy about some boy or other. But with you it's a little different; I guess she's hard hit. Now, that's the way I see it for her. How do I see it for you? And mind you, she'd take my head off if she thought that I was talking out of school.'

Mr. Ingram looked at the wide blue sky – the sun dazzled him. He looked at the ground – it was withering in the heat. He looked at the fat face of the blacksmith, and two keen eyes sparkled back at him.

'I didn't think –' he began.

'Try again,' said Vasa with a chuckle.

The blue eyes and the smile of Astrid flashed into the mind of the minister. Her smile was just a little crooked, leaving one cheek smooth, while a dimple came covertly in the other.

'I don't know,' said Ingram; 'as a matter of fact –'

'Only holding her hand?' said the blacksmith with a smile. 'Well, Ingram, I ain't throwin' her at your head. I'm just telling you to watch yourself. It don't take more'n five minutes for a girl like that to make a strong man pretty dizzy. And if she ever gets the right chance to work on you, I know Astie! She'll hit you with everything she's got, from a smile to a tear. She'll either have you on your knees worshippin', or else she'll have you comfortin' her. God knows what she would need comfort about! But that's the way she works. You understand? And one thing more – Red Moffet is wild about her. Red is the closest to a real man that's ever wanted to marry her. And he's got everything that her husband ought to have – money, grit, and sense. You've got sense. I guess you've got grit. But I know you ain't got money. Mind you, I'm just talkin' on the side. But, whichever way you're goin' to jump, you better make up your mind pretty quick. Because Red, if he don't hear something definite, is gunna lay for you with a gun one of these days!'

With this remark, Mr. Vasa arose.

'Girls are hell to raise,' said he, confidentially. 'Hell to have 'em and hell to lose 'em. Come on in, Ingram!'

'I'm busy at the church,' said Ingram, rather stunned.

'Has this here yarning cut you up some?'

'No, certainly not. I thank you for being so frank. I didn't, as a matter of fact –'

'Maybe I shouldn't have told you. Well, it's out, now, and it'll bring matters to a head. Whichever way you jump, good luck to you!'

They shook hands again, more gingerly. And Ingram turned out the gate and went up the street, his head low, and many thoughts spinning in his mind, like the shadows of a wheel. It was, of course, ridiculous that an Ingram should think of marrying a silly little Western girl.

And still, she was not so silly. File off a few rough corners of speech – she would learn as quickly as a horse runs – and –

He came to the church and stood before it, hardly seeing its familiar outlines. He had received counsel. But, oddly enough, what he wanted to do now was to go back and see Astrid and find out, first of all, if she really cared for him.

Suppose that she did; and that he was not ready to tell her that he loved her? He made a sudden gesture, as though to put the whole idea away from his mind, and with resolute face and firm step, he went into the church.

6

Talking Was His Business

A little chill went through Billman next day, for it was known that Red Moffet had discovered the name of at least one member of the posse that had hung Chuck Lane. Mr. Ingram heard the story from Astrid when she stayed a few moments after choir practice. It was a large choir, and though it was impossible to obtain enough male voices to match the sopranos, it was pleasant to hear the hymns shrilling sweetly from the throats of the girls.

Astrid stayed after practice and told the exciting tale. Mr. Red Moffet, by some bit of legerdemain, had secured the very rope with which Chuck Lane was hanged by the neck until dead. And, having secured that rope, Mr. Moffet had examined it with care and promptly recognized it. For, at the end, there was a queer little knot such as only a sailor would be likely to tie. And in Billman there was a cowpuncher and teamster who had been a sailor before the mast – one Ben Holman, a fellow of unsavory appearance. And worse reputation.

Red Moffet had, first of all, searched wildly through Billman to find the owner of that rope. But it was said that Mr. Holman heard that he was wanted and decided to look the other way. He slipped out from the village into the trackless desert. Mr. Moffet started in pursuit in the indicated direction, but straightway the desert became truly trackless, for a brisk wind rose, whipped the sands level, and effaced all signs.

Red Moffet came back to Billman, and the first place he went to was out to the cemetery, carrying the hangman's rope with him. He visited the most newly made grave and sat for a long time beside it. He himself had paid for the digging of that grave and for the headstone, which stood at one end of it, engraved in roughly chiseled letters:

'Here lies Chuck Lane. He was a good fellow that never played in luck!'

Men said that the inscription was Red's contribution also.

Whatever were the thoughts that passed through Moffet's mind as he sat there alone in the graveyard, Billman did not have the slightest hesitation in describing them as fluently as though Red had confided his ideas to the world in general.

'If you know what he was thinking, tell me,' suggested the young minister to Astrid.

'Oh, of course. Red was swearing that he would never give up the trail until he had Ben Holman's scalp.'

'Does he intend to murder that man for being one of the mob?' asked the minister.

'Murder?' echoed Astrid. 'Well, it isn't murder when you stick by a pal, is it?'

'This pal, as you call him, is already dead. And though the means used were illegal, I must say that it seems to me young Lane was not worthy of much better treatment than he received.'

At this, Astrid, who was sitting lightly on the back of a chair, swinging one leg to and fro, frowned.

'I don't follow that,' said she, 'You've got to stick by things, I suppose. Death doesn't matter, really.'

'But, Astrid –'

'I wonder,' broke in this irreverent girl, 'what folks would say if they heard me call you Reginald, or Reggie, say!'

'Why do you laugh, Astrid?'

'Why, Reggie is really a sort of a flossy name, isn't it?'

'It never occurred to me,' said that serious

young man. 'But to return to what you say – about death not mattering –'

'Between a man and his pal, I mean,' said Astrid. 'Why, you live after death, don't you?'

'Yes,' said Ingram. 'Of course.'

'Then,' said she triumphantly, 'you see the point. Even after a pal is dead, you'd want to do for him just what you'd do if he were living. That's pretty simple, it seems to me!'

'My dear child!' exclaimed he. 'What service is Red performing to Chuck Lane by chasing Ben Holman out of Billman and murdering him if he can?'

'Why, Reggie,' said the girl, 'how would you serve a friend, anyway? Suppose you're a friend of mine and you want music for your church. Well, I'd sing in your church, wouldn't I?' And she wrinkled her nose a little and smiled at him. 'Or suppose that I was a friend and that you wanted a new wing built on the church, I'd build it for you if I could, wouldn't I? Same in everything. You served a friend by doing what he would do for himself if he could, but which he can't –'

'I don't exactly see how you relate this to Red's murderous pursuit of Holman.'

'You don't? You're queer about some things, Reggie. Suppose that Chuck Lane could come back to earth, what would he want to do except turn loose and chase down the boys that strung him up? And first of all he'd want to get the fellow who loaned his rope to do the job. I think that's pretty clear!'

'Astrid, Astrid,' said Ingram, 'do you excuse a murder with a murder?'

'But it isn't murder, Reggie! Don't be silly! It's just revenge!'

' "Vengeance is mine, saith the Lord!" '

'Oh!' said she. 'Well, wait till the time comes, and I'll see how long you'd sit still and let a partner be downed by thugs or yeggs or something! You'd fight pretty quick, I guess!'

'No,' said he. 'Lift a hand against the life of a fellow? Astrid, we expressly are commanded to turn the other cheek!'

'Sure,' said Astrid. 'That's all right. But you can't let people walk over you, you know. Isn't good for 'em. Would make 'em bullies. You got to trip 'em up for their own sakes, don't you?'

'My dear Astrid, you are quite a little sophist!'

'And what does that mean?'

'A sophist is one who has a clever tongue and can make the worse way appear the better, or the better appear the worse.'

She grew excited.

'Suppose, Reggie, that you were to stand right here – you see? And a gun in your hand –'

'I never carry a gun,' said the minister mildly.

'Oh, bother! Just suppose! You're standing right

here with a gun in your hand, and your best friend is standing in the doorway of the church, and you see a greaser come sneaking in behind him with a knife – tell me, Reggie – would you let the greaser stick that knife into his back, or would you shoot the sneak – the low-down, yellow –'

'Such a thing could never happen here in the house of God,' said Ingram.

'Oh, but just supposin'! Just supposin'! Can't you even do a little supposin', Reggie? You make me tired, sometimes! I pretty nearly believe that you haven't got any real pals! Tell me!'

'Pals?' He echoed the word very gravely. And then his face grew a bit stern with pain.

'Hold on!' cried Astrid. 'I didn't mean to step on your toes like that. I see that you *have* got 'em, and –'

'No,' said he. 'There was a time when I had a good many friends. They were very dear to me, Astrid; but when I took up this new work, why, they drifted away from me. So many years – a very close life – books – study – a bit of devotion. No, I'm afraid that I haven't a single friend left to me!'

'That's terrible hard!' said the girl, sighing. 'But I'll bet you have, though. Look here, it makes you feel pretty bad, doesn't it, I mean the thought of having lost 'em?'

'I trust that I have no regrets for the small

sacrifices which I may have made in a great cause which is worthy of more than I could ever –'

'Stop!' cried Astrid. 'Oh, stop, stop! When you get humble like that, I always want to either cry – or beat you! I want to beat you just now! I say, you feel terrible bad because you've lost all those old friends. Then you can be sure that they feel bad to have lost you. So they still *are* your friends, and they would come jumping if you just gave them a chance! Tell me about them, Reggie.'

He shook his head.

'It is a little sad,' said he, 'to think of all the men who've been – well, I think I prefer to let it drop.'

'But I want to know. Look! I've told you everything about myself. And I don't know a thing about you. That's not fair. But the whole point is, that any real man would go to hell and back for the sake of a friend. Now wouldn't he?'

The minister was silent.

Astrid went on, innocent of having given offense: 'I'll tell you how it is, then, with Red. He and Chuck were old pals. Chuck's lynched. Well, Red wouldn't be a man worth dropping over a cliff if he wouldn't try to do something for his old partner. Isn't that clear and straight? I want to make you admit it.'

'I can't admit that,' said the minister slowly.

'By Jimminy!' said the girl, 'I *do* believe that you've never really had a hundred-per-cent friend

– the kind that they raise in this part of the country, I mean. A fellow who would ride five hundred miles for a look at you. Never write you a letter, most likely. But fight for you, die for you, swear by you, love you dead or livin', Reggie. That's the kind of a friend that I mean!'

The minister had bowed his head. He was silent; perhaps the torrent of words from that excited, small, round throat was bringing before his eyes all the men he had ever known.

'What are you seeing?' she asked suddenly.

'I'm seeing everything from the stubble field where the path ran to the swimming pool,' said Ingram sadly, 'to the empty lot behind the school where we used to have our fights; and the schoolrooms; and the men at college. Boys, I should say. They weren't men. They can't be men until they've learned how to endure pain!'

'Look here!' she snapped. 'Does a fellow have to suffer in order to be the right sort?'

'Would you trust something that looked like steel,' asked he, 'unless you knew it had been tempered by going through the fire?'

'Now you're getting a little highflown for me,' said the girl. 'It isn't only the men that have been your friends. But suppose I were to say that a girl you've known was in danger – the very one that you liked the most – suppose that she were standing there in the doorway, and a sneak of a

Mexican was coming up behind – what would you do? Would you shoot?'

'No, I would simply call: "Astrid, jump!" '

'I –' began Astrid.

Then the full meaning of this speech took her breath away and left her crimson. Ingram himself suddenly realised what he had said, and he stared at her in a sort of horror.

'Good gad!' said the Reverend Reginald Ingram, 'what have I said!'

'You've made me all d-d-dizzy!' said Astrid.

'I – as a matter of fact, the words – er – were not thought out, Astrid!'

'Of course you didn't mean –' began Astrid.

'I hope you'll forgive me!' said Ingram.

'For what?' she said.

'For blurting out such a –'

'Such a what?' she persisted.

'You're making it hard for me to apologize.'

'But I don't want you to apologize.'

'My dear Astrid –'

'I wish you'd stop talking so far down to me!'

'I see you're offended and angry.'

'I could be something else, if you'd let me,' said she.

'I don't understand,' said Ingram miserably.

'I could be terribly happy, if you meant what you said.'

He looked hopelessly about him. A daring blue

jay had lighted on the sill of the open window. Its bright, satanic eyes seemed to be laughing at him.

'You see – Astrid –'

'Don't!' cried she and stamped her little foot.

'Don't what?' he asked, more embarrassed than ever.

'Don't look so stunned. I'm not going to propose to you.'

'My dear child – the friendship which I feel – which – so beautiful – most extraordinary – fact is that – I don't seem to find words, Astrid.'

'Talking is your business,' said the girl. 'You've *got* to find words.'

'Do I?' asked Ingram, wiping his hot brow.

'You can't leave me floundering like this, unless it's because you have some sort of a doubt about me. I want to know. Tell me, Reggie!'

'What?' asked he, very desperate.

'You make me so angry – I could cry!'

'For Heaven's sake, don't! Not in the church, when –'

'Is that all you think about – your silly old church? Reginald Oliver Ingram!'

'Yes, Astrid!'

'Do I have to tell you that I love you?'

Mr. Ingram, sat down so suddenly and heavily that the chair creaked beneath his weight.

'Stand up!' ordered Astrid.

He stood up.

'You don't really care!' she cried.

'Astrid – I'm a bit upset.'

'Are you sick?'

'I'm a big groggy.'

'Reggie, cross your heart and tell me – have you ever been in love?'

'Not to my knowledge.'

'Never really been in love?'

'No.'

'Are you a little giddy and foolish and –'

'Yes.'

'You *are* in love!' said she.

'Do you think so?'

'Have you never proposed?'

'Never!'

'Never in your whole life – to any girl?'

'No!'

'Then you'd better begin right now.'

'Astrid, the thing is impossible!'

'What is?'

'To marry. You understand? I'm a minister. A poor man. Nothing but my salary –'

'Bother the silly salary! Do you want me?'

'Yes.'

'Honestly?'

'Yes.'

'More'n all the world?'

'Yes.'

'More'n all your old friends – almost as much as

your church and your work?'

'I think so,' said he.

'You'd better sit down,' suggested Astrid.

She took the chair beside him, and leaned her shining head against his shoulder.

'Heavens!' said Astrid.

'What's wrong?'

'How terribly happy I am! Why, Reggie, you're all trembling!'

'Because I'm trying to keep from touching you.'

'Why try?'

'We sit here in the house of God and in His presence, Astrid.'

'He would have to know some time,' said she. 'Gracious!'

'What, dear?'

'How hard you made me work!'

7
They Didn't Need Him

The ideas of Astrid about the practical problems of the future were extremely simple and to the point. They could easily live on his salary. How? All she wanted would be some horses for riding, and a few Mexican servants –

'I have just enough,' said he, 'to support one person on the plainest of fare, with no servant at all.'

'Oof!' said Astrid.

But after a little thought she arrived at another solution. She would simply tell her father that she needed enough money to marry on. And, of course, her father would give it to her.

'I couldn't marry you on another man's money,' said Ingram.

'But he isn't another man. He's my father.'

For answer, Ingram raised her hand to his lips, and felt it quiver as he touched it.

'I can see,' said Astrid, 'that I'll never be able to call my soul my own in our house! You're going to be a bully, Reggie!'

He smiled.

'But what *shall* we do?' she asked.

'Work – and wait – and I'll hope,' he began.

But she broke in: 'Of course it'll be arranged. You could go up in the hills and discover a mine or two, the way that father did. Reggie, that's a glorious idea! Because I'd really like to be rich. Wouldn't you? You could build such a wonderful big church then!'

Ingram studied her, half in awe and half in amusement, for heedless child and wise woman blended so oddly and unexpectedly in her that he never knew just how to take her.

However, having suggested that he take a flying trip to the mountains to make himself rich, she next felt that it might be better if no word of their engagement were given out for the moment.

'Chiefly because of dad,' said the girl. 'The minute you showed up, he said that I would throw over Red and marry you if I could. The silly old thing!'

'Has Red a claim on you?' asked Ingram.

'Red? Not a bit!'

'But you spoke of throwing him over?'

'Oh, right after the rodeo, you know. When Red had the prize both for riding and roping. Well, just about that time I saw a good deal of him, and I said that I'd marry him, some day, maybe!'

'As a matter of fact, you were definitely engaged to him?' asked Ingram sternly.

She turned and stared at him.

'What terrible rows we're going to have!' said Astrid Vasa. 'I hope we'll love each other enough to get through them safely. Sure – maybe you can say that I was engaged to him.'

'But you said before that he didn't have a whit of claim on you!'

'Oh, Reggie, don't pin me down. It's not fair, is it? You'd never doubt that I love you, Reggie? What did any other man matter to me after I once saw you?'

'Did you break your engagement with him?' asked the minister, clinging grimly to the point.

'You're going to be mean, I see,' sighed Astrid.

'Did you?'

'Of course, it's broken to tiny bits!'

'Before to-day?'

Her eyes were wide open, like the eyes of a child.

'Reggie – don't!' she begged.

'Then I'll go to tell him myself,' said Ingram.

'No!' screamed Astrid.

'No?'

'Don't go near him! He'd – he'd kill you, Reggie!'

'Would he murder me if I told him that you had become –'

'Don't even speak about it! It makes me see you lyin' dead! He told me he'd do it!'

'Told you that he'd do what?'

'He told me that he'd kill the other man, if I ever turned him down after once being engaged to him!'

'Did he actually tell you that – the ruffian?'

'Before he even proposed to me!' said Astrid.

'Ah?'

'He told me to think things over. Because he was going to ask me to marry him. He knew that I'd been engaged to other boys. He said that he wasn't a boy, but a man. And that he didn't expect to fall in and out with the girl he hoped to marry. It was to be all of him or none of him. And he said that if I ever drifted away from him, he'd stop me by putting a bullet into the gent that I was drifting toward. You understand, Reggie? Don't go near him, because he's a terrible fighter!'

Ingram made no promise. He watched Astrid walk down the street from the church; and he heard her gay voice sing out to a friend as she passed.

It left him to grave reflections. Old Vasa's first suggestion had utterly stunned him; but this dénouement, following so suddenly and unexpectedly, seemed to him most mysterious. It had been a matter of the moment. There was no reflection or planning. Words had burst from his lips of their own accord. And now he had placed himself in the hands of a little bright-haired girl of the desert, the daughter of a rude blacksmith and a simple household drudge.

He thought of the people among whom he had moved in other years, and his heart failed him. But when he thought of Astrid, his courage returned. For he felt that there was the right stuff in her. She had the right ring, and only bell metal makes the bell.

As for Red Moffet, he did not give that gentleman a serious second thought. Ingram returned to his little office beside the church and sat there for an hour, casting up accounts, going over papers, and with a mighty effort forcing out of his mind every concern except that of the church which he served.

Boxing teaches one to concentrate in a crisis; so does football; and the minister felt grateful to both sports as he worked in his little private room, with only the ghost of Astrid floating somewhere in the back of his brain.

It was very hot. But he had compunctions about taking off his coat while he was in any part of the sacred edifice. In fact Mr. Ingram was hopelessly medieval in many respects. And he kept himself stiffly incased in the armor of outworn ceremony.

However, the robes in which an idea is clothed are often essential to it; remove a man's manners, and you are apt to remove the man; and very few think of their prayers before they are on their knees. The gesture provokes the word, the word provokes the idea, and the idea may finally lead again to an act. So the young minister in his office kept himself rigidly in hand and would have been the last to guess that he did not use the formalities, but that the formalities used him.

In the midst of his labors, a tap came at his office door. He opened it and found himself facing Mr. Red Moffet. A dark scowl was upon the face of that gentleman, and according to the classic advice, he struck at once into the middle of his tale.

'Ingram,' said he, 'Billman don't need you. Astrid don't need you. I don't need you. You better move on before sunset!'

And with that brief remark, he turned and walked away, leaving the minister to stare after him blankly.

He had already heard of such warnings. Men who disregarded them usually fought for their lives before the next morning came – or else they accepted the advice and moved on.

What was he to do?

He had done his share of hunting; he had

worked with a revolver at a target in his time. But all of this was years ago and he was hideously out of practice, of course. Besides, he could not possibly use violent measures, even in self-defense. He could not imagine a more un-Christian proceeding.

What, then, was he to do?

He turned the thing backward and forward in his mind. Of course, he could not flee from the town. Of course, he could not ask for help from – from Vasa, say. But then, what remained to him to do?

He had felt that this was the very brightest and most joyous day in his entire life. But the brightness had been snatched away. No, not altogether! A thrill of happiness remained in his heart and never could be snatched away, save by her who had given it.

So, in a dark mood, indeed, he left his office and went back to his shack, where he paced up and down, wondering, probing a mind in which he knew he could find no suggestion of a solution for his difficulties. A great bitterness against Moffet swelled in his heart. For certainly it was unfair to attack one who was consecrated to peace and to peaceful ways. At another time – a few years before – when the clerical collar was not yet around his neck, he would not have been troubled by such a threat as he had received to-day. But those old days were gone, and his hands were tied!

But there was something of the ancient Roman in the minister. He had been placed at his post, and at his post he would stick, like those sentinels at Pompeii, who stood on guard until the ashes and the lava of Vesuvius buried them.

'Ah,' said a voice at his door, 'we still have our little yellow friend, eh? You've made him at home, Mr. Ingram, I see?'

He looked up and saw the black-robed Dominican before him. There was something so comfortable and reassuring in that brown, fat face, that Mr. Ingram fairly jumped from his chair to take the hand of the Mexican.

'Come in, Brother Pedrillo,' said he. 'Come in and sit down. I'm glad to see you!'

'Thank you,' said the other, and settling himself in the largest chair he turned to the lizard and whistled a thin, small note. Then he laughed, as the little creature lifted its head and listened.

'Look!' said the friar. 'You'd never think that he could move as fast as a whiplash, to see him now stiffened with the sun and a whistle, eh?'

Ingram made no comment. Small are the troubles of the man who can lose himself in the contemplation of a yellow lizard on a doorsill!

The friar turned back to him.

'I thought I could possibly be of help,' said he.

'Help?' asked Ingram, utterly at sea.

'Yes,' said the Dominican. 'I thought that I could help you pack.'

8

In the Hands of the Lord

It brought Ingram bolt upright.

'What do you know?' he asked.

'Know?' said the other, as though surprised by such a question. 'Oh, I know everything. I have to!'

'Will you tell me how?' asked Ingram.

'We Mexicans,' said the friar, 'are not like you Anglo-Saxons. Our tongues are connected directly with our hearts and our eyes. And so everything that we see or hear or feel must overflow in words – even the smallest things, you understand?'

'I don't see how that applies,' murmured Ingram.

'Think a moment, and you'll see the point,'

replied the brown friar. 'You don't know of the Mexicans in this town. You don't have to, because your work takes you to the Americans. But the Mexicans know you. For instance, some of them have been treated in your hospital –'

'It isn't mine,' said Ingram. 'I only suggested –'

'And planned, and begged and superintended, and collected the staff, and raised the money. Ah, we know, dear brother! All of those brown-skinned fellows who have been in the hospital have thanked the doctors, but they haven't forgotten you!'

Ingram stared. He had not foreseen such an eventuality when he planned the hospital.

'Those men are curious about you, of course,' said the friar. 'So they ask questions, they talk about you, and they find a few who can answer – a few of their own kind. The servants at the house of Señor Vasa – they are Mexicans, you understand? And though you have no Mexicans in your congregation, you have an old man to take care of the garden beside the church, and another to clean the place – well, they see! They have eyes and they know how to use them as quickly – as that lizard, say.'

'Well, what do they tell you?' asked Ingram impatiently.

'They tell me,' said the Dominican, 'that you, also, have eyes, brother, and that you know well how to use them.'

'That I don't understand,' replied Ingram.

'Ah,' said Pedrillo. 'Shall I be more open? The señorita is charming enough, surely. Can we not compliment you on –'

He paused, smiling.

'Oh, well,' said Ingram. 'There are no secrets in this town, I presume.'

'Also,' said the friar, 'a voice carries far in the silence of the desert. So I heard that perhaps you would be in a certain hurry, to-day!'

'Will the whole town know what Moffet said to me?'

'The town? Perhaps. The brown part of the town will, to be sure! You need not doubt that!'

'Tell me. What would you do if you were in my place, Brother Pedrillo?'

'I would not hesitate. I would pack at once and leave town before the sun set. I would be a comfortable distance away before the sun set, as a matter of fact.'

Ingram shook his head.

'You don't mean that,' he said. 'Having been assigned to a post, you wouldn't desert it!'

'That's a very harsh way of stating it,' said the friar. 'Suppose that I had no care about myself, still I would go.'

'Ah?'

'Because it would seem to me very wrong to

allow another man to commit a mortal sin in raising his hand against me. If you remain, Red Moffet must attack you. He has promised to do so. Nothing under heaven could keep him from fulfilling the obligation. That is the code by which he lives, of course. I understand it and, therefore, I should never place temptation in his way!'

'Run away from him?' asked Ingram. 'I couldn't do it!'

'Why?' asked the Dominican. 'Is it because you think it's wrong, or because you're a bit concerned about public opinion?'

Ingram raised his head.

'Public opinion? No!'

'I am afraid that you mean yes,' said Pedrillo.

'Well, perhaps I do. I don't want people to call me a coward!'

'Ah,' said the other, 'it's a hard time with you, I can see. To my more supple nature, the way would seem perfectly clear. But to you – no, that is different! I understand, however. Pride is a stubborn passion. And will it keep you erect in the face of this storm?'

'I trust that it will,' said Ingram.

'Well – then tell me what I can do for you, brother?'

'Nothing,' said Ingram. 'What *could* you do?'

'A great many things. Suppose that I let a word fall to a few of my compatriots in this town?'

'What of that?'

'A great deal might come of it. For instance, a number of them might call on Mr. Moffet in the middle of the night and urge him out of the town –'

The minister's nostrils flared with a burst of wicked passion, which he controlled with a strong and instant effort.

He recalled the powerful form of Moffet, his long, mighty arms. A gun sagged at either hip in a well-worn holster, polished not by hand, but by use.

'If they went to Moffet like that,' he said at last, 'some of them might be killed.'

The Dominican was silent.

'Some of them surely *would* be killed. Moffet would never go with them alive!'

'Perhaps not,' said Pedrillo. 'There is such a thing as duty which has nothing to do with pride, you see. Their duty would be to take him away so that he might be a danger to you no longer. His pride would force him to fight. What would come of it, who can tell? But much, for instance, may be done by a soft approach, and by the use of the rope. A rawhide lariat in the hands of one of my countrymen can be a knife, a club, or a tangling spider's web, strong enough to hold a struggling lion. Perhaps you had better let me send word to my friends!'

Ingram shook his head, more fiercely decided.

'This is my own fight,' said he, 'and I must see it through by myself. No other shall lift a hand on account of me!'

'You are familiar with guns, then?' asked the Dominican.

'I have been. But now I carry no weapons.'

'Here,' said the friar, 'is a chance for me to serve you. I shall bring you a revolver –'

'No,' said Ingram. 'The Gospel tells me what I must do in a case such as this. *Resist not evil*!'

'Our Lord,' said the Dominican, 'taught us by parables and seldom spoke directly. But He knew that He was not speaking to angels, neither was He speaking to devils. He wished us to interpret Him as a human being speaking to other human beings.'

Suddenly Ingram smiled.

'If you had twenty tongues,' said he, 'you couldn't persuade me! Thank you for coming.'

'I have failed then?'

'No, not failed. You have done what you could for me!'

'Then what will you do?'

'Pray,' said Ingram.

'Pray for Moffet, also,' said the friar. 'Because he is in danger of a frightful crime! Ah, brother, you have come very close to happiness in this place, and now I fear you are coming even closer to sorrow!'

'I am in the hands of the Lord,' said the minister, with a stern composure.

'And in the end,' said the Dominican, 'perhaps He will reveal to you the right way.'

He departed, wandering slowly from the door, pausing two or three times to turn back to his young friend as though there were still new arguments swelling up in his throat; but he seemed to decide that none of them would be of any avail, so stony had been the expression of Ingram.

After the friar had disappeared, Ingram looked across the roofs of the houses, with the heat waves shimmering up from them like steam, to the broad and burning plain of the desert.

He was seeing another picture in his mind's eye – of the bug eaten by the beetle, the beetle eaten by the wren, and the wren destroyed by the hawk. He began to wonder vaguely what order was maintained in this corner of the universe, and what topsy-turvy expression of the Divine Will was represented in it.

Then he turned from the doorway, flung himself on his blankets on the hard floor, and was presently asleep.

He wakened with a singing in his ears, for it had been very hot.

He staggered to the door. It was still breathless, no wind was stirring, and the ground and the houses poured out as from the mouths of ovens the heat which they had been drinking in all day. Twilight had thickened and the night was coming on rapidly, but a dim band of fire still circled the horizon as if with an ominous promise that, as the day had been, so would the morrow be also.

Ingram washed his face and hands. Supper was not thought of. He had been warned to leave the town that day before sunset, and the sun already had set!

Now what would happen?

He forced himself to go methodically about his business. He was conscious of a vast, craven desire to flee from the house and hide in some dark corner, but he fought back the impulse sternly. He lighted a lamp, trimmed the wick, saw that it was burning brightly and evenly, and then sat down with a book.

The print blurred and ran togther. He could not make sense of the thing that lay before his eyes.

Then he mastered himself again, with such a vast effort that sweat not brought by heat poured down his forehead. The words cleared. He began to take in the author's meaning.

And then a voice called strongly from the street: 'Ingram!'

He recognized it at once as the voice of Red Moffet. Yonder he stood in the dark of the public way. Perhaps others were gathered covertly to watch the tragedy.

The minister stepped into the doorway.

A lamp was burning at a window just across the street, and against that lamp he saw the silhouette of the horseman.

'I am here,' said Ingram.

Then something whistled over his head. He was gripped by the powerful clutch of a slip noose, and jerked from his feet as Red Moffet began to ride down the street, dragging his victim through the thick dust behind him.

9

Keeping the Secret

He was half stifled when the dragging ceased; and suddenly he was trundled by skillful hands in a net of stout rope. He could not move hand or foot, and was brought by main force and tied to a sapling.

No one was near. Billman was lost in darkness. The town was at its evening meal, and Moffet had chosen the most convenient hour to work without interruption.

Deftly Moffet removed the minister's shirt.

He stepped back.

'I'm gunna give you a lesson that ought to last you a while, you skunk!' said Red Moffet. 'If you was a man, I'd shoot daylight out of you. But bein' only a minister, I got to do this!'

And a riding quirt sang in his hand and

branded the back of the minister with fire.

A dozen strokes, but not a sound from the victim.

'Fainted, eh?' grunted Moffet.

He lighted a match.

Blood was trickling down Ingram's white back. He walked around and by the light of the match Moffet stared into such eyes as he never before had seen in any human being.

He dropped the match with an oath.

Then he said in the darkness: 'That'll teach you. But if I catch you in Billman to-morrow, I'll handle you worse'n this!'

And he rode away, the thick dust muffling the sound of his horse's hoofs.

Against that tree the minister leaned all night. Exhaustion overcame him; but the cutting ropes which bound him held up the weight of his body; and burning rages of shame and hate sustained him until, in the crisp chill of the desert morning, men found him there and cut him down.

He fell like a log, unconscious. They carried him back to his house and gave him a drink of whisky. One grim-faced cow-puncher said to him, half sneering and half in pity: 'You better get out of town, Ingram, before Moffet does worse'n this to you!'

Ingram made no reply. His nerves were so completely shattered that he dared not open his lips for fear anything from a sob to a scream might come from them.

He lay trembling until the mid-morning.

Then he got up, stripped away his tattered clothes, and washed his swollen, wounded back. He remembered suddenly that it was Sunday morning, and that a sermon should be preached in half an hour.

So he walked to the church with a steady step – and found not a soul there!

Not even the Mexican to ring the bell! He rang it himself, long and loudly, and then went back into the church and waited.

No one came. The little church through its open doors drank in some of the sultry heat of that bitter day, but no human being crossed its threshold until long after the sermon should have begun.

Ingram wondered if it was a sense of delicacy which held back the crowd of women who should have been there?

And then into the church walked no woman, but the tall, lumbering giant, Vasa. He came up to the minister and sat down beside him.

Pity and wonder were in Vasa's glance, but withering scorn predominated over them.

'I got a note from sis for you,' said he, and tendered an envelope.

It was amazingly brief and to the point.

It merely said: 'How could you lie down and let any man do that to you? I'm ashamed and I'm sick. Go away from Billman. No one will ever want to see your face here again!'

No signature even. The words were enough. And the splotches and smudges which covered the paper – well, they were a sign of tears of bitterest shame and disgust, no doubt. He folded the paper carefully and put it into his pocket.

'I'd better be going,' said Vasa.

And he stood up. He added suddenly: 'Darned if I ain't sorry, Ingram. I didn't think you were the sort that would let any –'

He stopped himself, turned upon his heel and was gone. Ingram closed the church and went home again.

Delicacy which had kept the women from the church that morning? There was no more delicacy in Billman and its people than there was in the birds and the insects of the desert around them. They were walled away from him now by the most profound contempt.

By the middle of the afternoon, he knew what he must do, and he walked down to the telegraph office. He met a hundred people on the way, but not a single pair of eyes. They turned away when they saw him coming. They slipped this way and that so that they might not have to encounter him. Only a pair of boys ran out of a gate and after him, laughing, yelling, calling out words suggested to them by the fiend that inhabits boys.

At the telegraph office he wrote a telegram:

> My usefulness at Billman ended; suggest that you send a new man and an old one for this post; will wait till his arrival if necessary.

He signed that message and directed it to those who had dispatched him on this distant mission. Then he walked back down the street towards his shack once more.

He wanted to hurry, but he made himself walk with a deliberate step. He wanted to skulk around the backyards to get to his destination, but he checked himself and held on his way through the thick of men and women. More boys came out to mock at him. And he heard a mother sharply scold her offspring.

'Let the poor, good-for-nothin' creature alone, can't you, boys?'

That was for him!

He got to his shack again, and remembered suddenly for the second time that day that it was the Sabbath. So he took up his Bible and began to read, forcing his eyes to consider the words until a shadow fell through the doorway and across the floor to his feet.

It was the Dominican.

He came in and held out his hand. Ingram failed to see it.

Then Brother Pedrillo said: 'I guessed at a good many things, brother. But this thing I didn't guess at. I thought that it would be simply a matter of guns. I didn't imagine that it could be anything worse!'

He added, after a moment: 'Brother, I understand. The rest have not seen the truth. You hate them now. Afterward, you will remember that they are like children. Forgive them if you can. Not to-day. It would be too hard. But to-morrow.'

This he said, and afterward withdrew as quietly as he had come, and went down the street with a fat man's waddling step.

In due time, he passed Vasa's house, and found the busy matron in the garden, snatching a moment from her housekeeping to improve the vegetables. He leaned on the picket fence to talk with her.

'And how's Astrid?'

'That girl's in bed,' said Mrs. Vasa. 'Pretty sick, too.'

'Sick?' queried the friar. 'What does the doctor say about it?'

'Oh it ain't a thing for doctors to know about. Doctors ain't much help sometimes, brother.'

Pedrillo wandered on down the street. He

passed the hotel, where he was hailed jovially by the idlers, and drinks of various kinds and sizes, were suggested. He refused them all, not that he was above having a glass of beer – or pulque as the case might be – but because he drank in a house, not in a saloon. And at the farther corner of the hotel he fairly ran into Red Moffet.

Red hailed him. The friar walked on in silence, and the tall cow-puncher instantly was at his side.

'Look here, Pedrillo. What's the matter? Didn't you see me?'

'I don't want to talk to you, Red,' said the friar. 'Because if I start talking, my temper may get the best of me.'

'You mean Ingram, I suppose,' said the big fellow.

'I mean Ingram.'

'Well, what would you have me do? Use a gun on him instead?'

'May I tell you what I think, Red?'

'Fire away, old fellow. *You* can say whatever you please.'

'Then I'll tell you what I firmly believe – that if a scruple didn't stand in his way, Ingram could thrash any two men in this town!'

'What kind of a joke is that?' asked Moffet.

'It's not a joke, but the coldest kind of hard fact.'

'Why, brother, the man's yellow!'

'Don't tell me that, Red. He's simply keeping

himself in hand. He won't fight on principle – not for the sake of his own hide. And just now, you are on the crest and he's in the trough. But I shouldn't be surprised if he turned the tables on you one of these days!'

'He'll have to make it quick,' said Red. 'The quitter has had enough. He's wired to be taken from the town.'

'Has he done that?'

'Yep, he's hollered for help.'

And Red grinned with malicious content.

'Very well,' said the Dominican. 'He's asking to be relieved because he thinks he no longer can do good here – after the way you disgraced him. But I'll tell you, Red, that this is going to be no short story for you. It is apt to be a very, very long one!'

He went on without further words, and with a very dark brow, leaving Red Moffet deep in thought behind him.

On across the creek to the poorer section of the town went the friar, until he found himself in the quarters of his compatriots. There the theme was the same as that which occupied the Americans in the more prosperous section of Billman.

And a lame fellow fresh from the hospital said to the Dominican: 'Our friend, Señor Ingram, he is not much of a man, brother?'

'Who has told you that?' snapped Pedrillo.

'Look! He has been whipped like a dog!'

'Shall I tell you a thing, my friend?'

'Yes.'

'It is a great secret, amigo.'

'Then tell me, brother.'

'This Señor Ingram is a quiet man. But also when the time comes, it will be seen that he is *muy diablo*.'

There is no way to translate that phrase – *muy diablo*. It means 'much devil' or 'very devil'. And then it has other meanings as well. One can say that a maverick is *muy diablo*. Also one may use the expression concerning a stick of dynamite. The peon listened to the friar and opened his eyes. Never for a moment did it occur to him to doubt.

'I shall keep the secret!' said he. 'But when will Señor Ingram act?'

'That is with God and his conscience. He will act in good time!'

And he watched the peon hurry away. He knew that in half an hour the whole town would be apprised of the secret that Señor Ingram, the minister, in some mysterious way, was *muy diablo*. Brother Pedrillo was content.

10
The Mystery of Work

Rumor in Billman, as in all small Western towns, moved with the speed and the subtlety of a serpent. And so the tale rapidly went the rounds that Ingram, despite his fall at the hands of Red Moffet, was stronger than he seemed to be; that he was, in fact, *muy diablo.* He was biding his time. Before long, something would happen to reveal him to the people as he was in truth.

The cow-punchers, hearing the tale, shrugged their shoulders and were inclined to laugh. But afterward, they remembered and pondered the matter. There had been something in the unflinching manner with which big Ingram walked their streets the very day after his disgrace that gave them pause. They turned the matter in their minds and became more serious.

The story came to the ears of Astrid Vasa and made her sit up suddenly in bed, her eyes shining.

Who could tell?

In five minutes she was dressed. In five minutes more she was on the street, hurrying to Ingram.

She found him in his shack, with a telegram in his hand, which told him that there was no possibility of replacing him at once in Billman, and that he would have to remain at his post for an indefinite period. In the meantime, he must write all details of what had happened.

When Astrid called, he came out into the sun and stood there with his head lowered and thrust forward a little, like a fighter prepared to receive a blow. She was abashed.

So she stood by the gate, guiltily hoping that no one would see her there.

'I only wanted to say, Reggie, that I wrote that note without thinking. I hope that I didn't hurt you – I mean – I thought –'

He lifted his eyes to her face. Astrid uttered a little cry.

'I should never have written it!' she pleaded. 'I'm sorry. And I didn't know that you would – that you –'

And she added suddenly: 'Won't you say something?'

No, not a word. She did not feel that his was the sulky silence of a child. Rather it was a considerate silence, as of a man who needs a quiet moment for thinking. But it was as though she were thrust away from him by a long arm. It was as though she never could have been near him.

Astrid began to regret, and to regret bitterly. Not that she knew just what was in the mind of Mr. Ingram, or what he was as a man – but that she felt he was something different from any other man who had ever been in Billman. And Astrid loved novelties!

'You won't forgive me!' moaned Astrid suddenly.

'Forgive you?' repeated the deep voice. 'Oh, yes, I forgive you!'

No passion in it. No more than if he were reading the words out of a book, and somehow that was more to Astrid Vasa than the bitterest denunciation. She shrank away down the street and hurried to her home.

Her father was not there.

She rushed to his shop, and there she found him. The forge was sending up masses of smoke, for the fuel had just been freshened; smoke wreathed all the shadowy cave in which the forge flame was darting like a snake's tongue. In the midst stood Vasa, his shirt off, the top of his hairy chest and his wonderful arms, loaded down with muscles, exposed. He had donned a leather apron. In one hand he swayed a fourteen-pound sledge tentatively.

'Dad!' cried Astrid, 'I want to speak to you!'

'Hey – you! Get out of here!' called her father fiercely.

She had walked into the grime and the heavy, impure air. And with the unceremonious wave of his arm her father sent her staggering back to the door.

She was furious, for no human being ever had treated her after this fashion. Not since she had first been called by her full name of Astrid.

She saw the two assistants bear the great beam of iron from the forge fire, each of them toiling with a pair of huge pincers. She saw the beam laid across the anvil. Then the sledge in the hands of her father began to sweep through the air in rapid circles, and at each stroke a thousand rays of liquid fire darted to every corner of the shop, lighting up all its cobwebbed angles and showing the smoke, thick as milk, which hovered against the beams of the roof.

The assistants winced under those showers of sparks and shrank away; the blows fell more rapidly. She heard her father bellowing orders, and saw the iron being turned, moved here and there on the anvil according to his directions. And then, half disgusted and half afraid, she saw that all this noise and smoke and fury was merely for the sake of putting a bend in that massive bit of iron, a right-angle bend, and also to round the iron about the angle point.

Then she saw her father seize the iron beam with one pincers and with one hand plunge it into the tempering tub. With one hand – that burden for two strong men!

There was a frightful hissing, as though a vast cauldron filled with rattlesnakes had been threatened with death. A billow of steam rolled out and all within the shop was lost in fog. At length, parting the mist before him with his hand, Vasa came toward Astrid and towered above her.

'Well, honey, what you want?'

She did not answer. She only stared.

'I was kind of rough, Astie, dear,' said he. 'Don't be mad with me!'

It was not his roughness that amazed her, but his sudden gentleness. And Astrid began to guess at vastly new thoughts, and vastly large ones. That bending of the iron in itself was not so important, perhaps. The iron would become a part of a stupid machine. But what *was* important was that a man with fire and hammer to aid him had turned that strong iron as though it had been wax, melted and molded it, and given it a new shape!

So thought Astrid. And she could understand the roughness with which her father had greeted her. For she had come between him and his work – that mystery of work! She had been nothing –

merely an annoyance! She had felt, before this, that nothing so important as herself could come into the life of some chosen man. But now she guessed that the more worth while the man, the more his work would mean to him, and the less the winning of a woman. Would she, then, be pushed into the background? Was it right?

Right or wrong, with terrible suddenness the girl realized that she never could care truly for any man save for one capable of elevating his labor into a god in this fashion. Even if it were no more than the shaping of iron beams. Yes, even that work could be great and important if it were approached in the right manner. And it was this which gave a certain surety and significance to her father. He was all that she had ever thought him – gross, careless, slovenly – but also worthy of respect.

So thought Astrid, and accordingly she greeted her father as she never had greeted him before, with a touch of awe.

'Can you spare me a minute, dear dad?' she said.

'A minute?' he asked, amazed. 'Sure, kid! Or an hour; now what you want? What's botherin' you? You look sort of upset!'

He took her by the elbows and lifted her to the top of a great packing case. She would have cried out, at another time, because his hands were smudging her dress. But now she merely smiled down at him, a rather uncertain, frightened smile.

'You tell your old dad!'

'You remember that note you took to Reggie Ingram?'

'Aye, I remember.'

'I told him in that note – that I didn't have any more use for him!'

'Hello! That was kind of hard!'

'Dad, I'd got myself engaged to him before that.'

'You did!'

'And then I threw him over.'

'What else could you do? A gent that lets himself –'

'No!'

He was silent.

'You tell me, then,' he said at last.

'I want him back! Dad, you got to get him back for me!'

Mr. Vasa combed his hair with fingers covered with the black of iron.

'What am I gunna do, honey? Get down on my knees and beg him to marry you after all? Look here, I'll bring him to the house. You got to do the rest; but, sis, ain't you a little crazy to want to take a man that's been –'

'No!' cried she.

He was silent again. And she wondered that with all his force he should submit so easily to her desires. It was as though he felt that her intelligence was worth more than his in this affair.

'I can't talk to him!' said Astrid, with a sob. 'I've just been to see him and tried, but he only looked at me and said nothing until I asked him to forgive me, and then he said that he would; but he's put me out of his life – and I can't stand it! I can't stand it, dad!'

'So? So?' murmured the big blacksmith.

He lifted her down to the ground and dried her eyes.

'I'm gunna do what I can,' said he. 'But, I dunno! It looks pretty bad. Though there's a yarn going around the town that after all he's not what we think – that this Ingram is *muy diablo*, sis. Have you heard that?'

She answered fiercely: 'You wait and see! You wait and see!'

Vasa nodded, and she went slowly back home.

It had been a day of wreckage and disaster to her old idea, and the new idea was not yet firmly established in her mind, so she felt weak, and frightfully uncertain. She only guessed that there were such forces loose in the world of men as she never before had dreamed of.

And then, at the door of her home, she met Red Moffet, who was grinning, and looking both shamefaced and proud of himself, like a child that expects to be praised.

She shrank from him.

'I've got a headache; I can't talk to you, Red,' she told him truthfully enough. 'I've got to be alone!'

And she walked straight past him.

Now Red was a man among men, and he was intelligent enough to prospect for gold-bearing ore, and find it and work it. But he did not understand the ways of women. Men usually are like that. The more brave and bold and successful they are in their own fields, the more obtuse, clumsy and inept they are with the women who enter their lives. Perhaps there never was a universal favorite with women who was not a bit effeminate, or something of a charlatan. One needs a dainty touch with women. A conversation with them is like a surgical operation upon nerves. The slightest slip of the hand or a cut a shade too deep and the result is total failure. The light-tongued jugglers of words – they are the successful ones.

But poor Red did not know this.

All that he was sure of was that he loved this girl, and that he felt he had eliminated from the competition his one dangerous rival. But instead of reaping the fruits of victory, he was received with open weariness and disgust.

So he followed her to the door and even touched her shoulder.

She whirled around at him, shrinking as if his touch were a contamination.

'I want to know,' began Red, 'what's happened to make you so very –'

'You bully!' she cried.

It staggered Red, and he fell back.

'Bully?' he said, amazed.

'You cowardly, great, hulking, worthless bully!' cried Astrid, following him.

He could not stand his ground. He retreated through the door, forgetting his hat.

She threw it after him.

'I hope I never see you again!' cried Astrid.

11

'Without Losing No Dignity'

Nothing offends us so much as the illogical. We do not demand a great deal from the world. But we wish for our logical rewards – and a little bit more. If a child has cut up your best hat in order to make an ash tray for you, you must not scold him, no matter how your heart is bleeding. He expects a bit of praise, and praise he must have. Or if you point out to him, with care, that he has been in most frightful error and really deserves a whipping, then he is mortified, ashamed, shrinks from you, and presently hates the entire world.

This was exactly the frame of mind of young Red Moffet. He had seen an Easterner, a tenderfoot, a minister, walk into Billman and promise to carry away the prettiest girl in the entire town. He had stopped that proceeding with the might of his good right arm, and now all glory, all reward was denied him!

He jammed his hat upon his head and set his teeth. He was, indeed, furious enough to have torn out the heart of his best friend and thrown it to the dogs.

He was known in Billman, was young Red Moffet. And when he was in such a humor, it would have been hard to hire a man to cross his way. But Fate, who insists on shuffling the cards and dealing the oddest hands, now drew the worst deuce in the pack and presented it to Red Moffet.

For Ben Holman had come back to town that day. He had been angered by the wrath of Red Moffet; and since he was only one third wild cat and two thirds sneak, he had vowed to himself that never would he cross the path of that dreadful destroyer of men. There had been sundry killings in the past of Ben Holman himself, but always he had shot or knifed from behind. That allowed him to take better aim and keep a cooler head. Whereas, when he stood confronting another puncher who wore a gun, he discovered at once that his heart was out of sorts.

But now the good news came to him that Red

had put down the minister, for the reputed reason that the minister needed putting down if Red was to keep his girl, pretty Astrid Vasa. Ben Holman knew Astrid by sight and he felt that the man who had won her back would be so completely happy that he would forget all past enmities – even his hatred of those who had officiated at the killing of poor Chuck Lane.

At any rate, Ben was something of a gambler, the kind who always like short odds. And what odds could be shorter than these? He determined to return to Billman and try his luck in appeasing Mr. Red Moffet before a gun could be drawn on him.

These were the reasons which drew Ben back to the town. They were good reasons; they were well thought out; they were well founded. If he had come half an hour earlier, all would have been well.

But at this very worst of moments, as he turned the corner of the street, young Red Moffet came straight upon Holman, riding toward him and not twenty feet away.

There was no time for thinking. Holman screeched like a frightened cat and whipped out his gun with the desperation of any cornered wild thing. He actually got in the first shot, and it lifted the hat of Red Moffet and sent it sailing into the air. Red Moffet got in the second shot. And he did *not* miss. His bullet struck Ben Holman in the throat, tore his spinal column in two, and dropped him in a shapeless heap on the farther side of his horse. Then Red Moffet went out with his smoking gun and saw what he had done.

He felt no pangs of conscience. He was merely relieved, and sighed a little, as though he had got something out of his system. Then he straightened out his victim, put the latter's sombrero over his face, and hired half a dozen passing Mexicans to carry Ben to the burying grounds just outside the village.

Perhaps twenty men had been interred there under similar circumstances. Red Moffet had sent two there himself. But since he had always paid the price of the ground and the price of the burial, nothing had been said, and this time he expected not the slightest trouble.

He had simply done his duty by Chuck Lane – that thorough, good fellow – and having eased his conscience, what call was there for any further excitement about the matter?

But Fate, as has been said, is a tricky lady who loves to mix the cards and deal the unexpected. There was hardly a soul in Billman who cared whether Ben Holman lived or died. His reputation was not much more savory than the reputation of a coyote, or any other sneaking beast of prey. And every one knew that Red Moffet shot from in front, waited for the other man to fill his hand, and was, in addition, a hardworking and honest member of the community. However, it happened that Red had, in fact, turned this trick before. And there is nothing more annoying to an audience than to have an actor return to the stage to sing his song over again when there has been no applause to warrant an encore. Red's last shooting exploit was hardly three months old. And the news about Holman's death touched the nerves of Billman's citizens in a sensitive spot.

Killing in the cow-country is a diversion to be forgiven any man now and then. But it should never be allowed to become a mere habit.

It looked as though Red had formed the habit.

More than this, hardly twenty-four hours ago he had manhandled the minister. When you come to think of it, the said minister had done no harm. As a matter of fact, he had been a useful and quiet member of the community. Reputations die quickly in a mining town, as elsewhere. But Ingram had built that hospital very recently. And there were a number of convalescents around the town at that moment. They did not take kindly to the roughing of their benefactor. And now they listened somberly to this new tale of violence.

A Western town usually makes up its mind quickly. As a matter of fact, often it doesn't stop to make up its mind before it acts.

Now Dick Binney, the deputy sheriff, had no love for Red Moffet. But he knew Red and he knew Ben Holman, and he no more thought of arresting the former for the killing of the latter than he would have thought of arresting a man for the killing of a prowling wolf on the streets of the town.

Eight tall, strong, brown-faced men strode into Dick's office and sat down in his chairs, on his desk, and in the window.

'Dick,' they said, 'we reckon that maybe you better put Red up where he'll be safe to cool off for a while. He's runnin' up the death rate near as bad as smallpox.'

Dick Binney looked from one face to another, and after a few moments' thought he nodded.

'Boys,' said he, lying cheerfully, 'I was thinking the same thing.'

He got up and left his office, and the big men followed him at a distance. The deputy came on Red Moffet, cheerfully chucking stones at a squirrel which was up a tree.

'Red,' said he, 'I hate to do this, but I got to ask you to come along with me.'

While he spoke, he tapped Red lightly on the shoulder.

'Come along with you where?' asked Red savagely. 'What you talkin' about, man?'

'To jail, for a rest,' said the deputy sheriff.

'To jail?' said Red Moffet. 'What's the funny idea?'

And he added vigorously: 'For what?'

'For the killing of Ben Holman.'

'It's dirty work on your part,' said Red Moffet in anger. 'You know that Holman has been due to be bumped off for a long time, and the only thing that saved him was that nobody wanted to waste a bullet on an insect like him.'

'Sure,' agreed the deputy. 'You never said nothin' truer. Matter of fact, Red, I ain't been no friend of yours, but I would never have arrested you for killin' Ben. Only, public opinion, it sort of demands this.'

'Public opinion can go hang,' said Red.

'Sure,' grinned Dick Binney. 'But when there's eight public opinions wearing guns, all of 'em, it's sort of different, don't you guess?'

He hooked a thumb in the proper direction, and Red Moffet became aware of eight good men and true, in various careless attitudes. Red had a practiced eye, and with one glance he counted eleven revolvers and three rifles. Those were the weapons which were displayed for public notice. Undoubtedly there were others concealed.

'Well,' agreed Moffet, 'it looks like you got some reason in what you say. Maybe I'll come along with you!'

Down the street they went.

'This is gunna be talked about, Dick,' said Red Moffet. 'It's gunna be said that I'm no good, if I let myself be arrested without strikin' a blow.'

Dick Binney, walking beside him, nodded in ready agreement.

'That's true,' said he. 'I hadn't thought about that.'

Red halted.

'I'm afraid,' said he, 'that I can't let you take me without shooting for the prize, old-timer.'

'Hold on, Red,' said the deputy sheriff, 'if I was to kill you just now – hatin' your innards the way I do and me being sheriff – it would be all right. But if you was to kill me – well, you know how things go with a gent that kills a sheriff?'

Red Moffet nodded gravely.

'I know,' said he. 'You sure are playing the part of a white man to me to-day, Dick. If I didn't hate you for a low skunk, I'd figure you to be one of the best.'

'I'll shoot your innards out, one of these days,' said Binney, 'but I ain't gunna take advantage of you now. I'll tell you what I'll do. I'll put a hand on your shoulder. You knock it off. I'll make a pass at you with my fist and we'll close and grapple and start fighting as though we'd forgot all about our guns. Y'understand? The rest of the boys'll think that you're resisting arrest. They'll come runnin' up and you can afford to give up to eight armed men without losing no dignity.'

'Sure,' agreed Red Moffet. 'Dick, I pretty near love you when I see what a wonderful head you got on your shoulders!'

With that, Dick clapped a hand upon the shoulder of his companion. The hand was promptly knocked off; and Mr. Binney made the promised pass at his companion with his fist. However, he did not merely fan the air. He had a hard and ready fist and he cracked it squarely along the side of Mr. Moffet's jaw. The hair rose on the crown of Red's head. 'You hound dog!' he grunted.

And with that, he lifted a hearty uppercut from his toes to the chin of the deputy sheriff.

It was only by good luck that the deputy did not fall on his back. If he had done so, eight good men and true who were rushing down the street toward the fighters would have shot Red so full of holes that he would have looked in death like nothing but a colander. But by happy chance the deputy sheriff fell in and not out. He pitched into the arms of Red, who caught and held him, and they pretended to wrestle back and forth, the deputy sheriff groaning: 'You hit me with a club, you sap!'

In the midst of this struggling, the rescue party arrived, and quantities of guns were shoved under Red's nose. He pushed his hands into the air with a reluctance which was only partly assumed.

'You seem to have the drop on me, boys,' said Red. 'What might you be wanting of me? A invitation to call, or something like that?'

'He ought to get what Chuck Lane got, the darned man-killer,' said one harsh voice. 'Resists arrest, and everything! Lucky that we were on deck!'

'Lucky nothing!' declared the deputy sheriff, who was able to walk without staggering at about this moment. 'I was beating him to a pulp for my own pleasure before lockin' him up. Come along to the jail, Red, or I'll knock your block off!'

So, with a volunteer guard of honor, Red was escorted down the street and installed in the jail of which Billman was so proud. He was given the most comfortable quarters that the little building could afford, and Binney sat down outside his door and chatted with him, tenderly rubbing his jaw the while.

'When you get out of this, Red,' said the deputy sheriff, 'I'm gunna beat you to a fare-thee-well!

But in the meantime, I'll try to make you comfortable here!'

12

The Seventh Day

It is so unpleasant to dwell on the miseries which beset the mind of young Ingram, that we may skip to the moment when Vasa leaned against the post of his door, saying: 'Hello, Ingram! Here I am back again. Am I welcome?'

There was an uncertain murmur from Ingram in reply.

'No,' declared the unabashed giant, 'I can see that I ain't, but still I ain't downhearted. I can't afford to be. But the fact is, old man, that you've cut up my girl a good deal. I've had to come along and try to make peace with you for her sake. What chance do you think I have?'

'Peace? With me?' asked the minister bitterly. 'But of course, that's a jest. I am a man of peace, Mr. Vasa. I thought that I had proved that to the entire town!'

The blacksmith felt the bitterness in this speech. He could think of nothing better to say than: 'Well, Ingram, folks are getting pretty sorry for what's happened. I suppose you know what they've done to Red Moffet just now?'

'I don't know,' said the minister, turning pale at the mere sound of the man's name.

'They've locked him up in jail! For what he done to you – and for killing Ben Holman!'

'Did he kill a man?' asked the minister slowly.

'Shot him dead.'

'However,' said Ingram, 'it was in fair fight, I presume?'

'What made you guess that?' asked the blacksmith.

'Because I thought that he was that kind of a man.'

'As a matter of fact, you're right. It was a fair fight. And that Holman was a hound. But still – we've stood for too much from Red. He's got to have a lesson. But I thought that I'd ramble up here and ask you about sis. Are you through with her for good and all, Ingram?'

The minister was silent.

'Think it over,' suggested Vasa. 'That girl is all fire and impulse. She's probably got ten ideas a minute, and nine out of the ten are wrong. Think it over, and let her know later on what you decide.'

'Thank you,' said Ingram.

Mr. Vasa felt very uncomfortable. He began to perspire freely, and finally he stood up and left. He hurried down the street as though to leave a sense of unpleasantness as far as possible in the rear.

Reginald Ingram was not cheered by this embassy. He had fallen so far into the deeps of shame that he felt nothing could bring him back to self-respect. But now he began to torment himself in a new manner. Red Moffet was in jail. Was it his duty as a Christian to go to see his enemy?

The thought made him writhe. And in the midst of his writhings, Friar Pedrillo appeared. He was filled with news and, in particular, he could detail all that had happened concerning the arrest of Moffet.

'The evil are punished,' said the Dominican. 'And now Red Moffet is crouching in jail in fear of his life.'

'Do you think that they would hang him for what he has done?' asked Ingram, half sad and half curious.

'Not by process of law,' replied the friar. 'They can't convict him with a Billman jury for having killed Ben Holman, who was a known scoundrel. But there is another danger for poor Red.'

'Another danger?'

'Yes, of course. There's the mob you know.'

'I don't understand.'

'You will, if you go downtown this evening. There's a whisper going about the town, and I think that after dark there will be a good many people grouping around the jail and planning to take Red out and hang him up.'

'Wait a moment,' cried Ingram. 'I thought that Red Moffet was popular in this town?'

'Six days a week, he is,' said the Dominican. 'But on the seventh you may find his enemies in the saddle, and this seems to be the seventh day.'

With that, Brother Pedrillo left, and Ingram found himself plunged into a melancholy state in which he was lost for the remainder of the day.

But when the evening drew on, he knew what he must do. He must go to the jail and be near when the crisis came. Exactly what prompted him to go, he could not tell. He could not honestly say that he wished big Moffet well. And yet –

As he walked down the street, he told himself that he would, at any rate, try to do what he could for the prisoner, in case of mob violence. When he reached the vicinity of the jail, he found a swarm of people of all sorts and all ages. And every one of them had one topic on his lips – the name and the fate of Red Moffet, who was now waiting in the jail for his end.

The minister went through the crowd like a ghost; it seemed that no one had eye or ear for him. He was an impalpable presence, not worthy of being noticed.

It was a strange crowd, gathering in little knots here and there, talking in deep, grave voices. Now and again, Ingram heard some louder, more strident voice. When he listened, it was sure to be some one recalling some evil act on the part of Moffet, some episode in Red's past which had to do with guns and gore.

The minister went to the jail, where he found the door closed and locked. When he knocked, a subdued voice inside said: 'It's the minister. It's Ingram.'

'Let him in, then,' said another voice.

The door was opened just enough for him to slip through and, as he did so, there was a rush from the street behind him. But the door was swung shut with a crash, before any one got to the spot.

Outside there were curses loud and long, and a beating on the door by men who demanded entrance at once.

Inside, Ingram found the deputy sheriff and two others, a pale-faced group, who looked gloomily at him.

'What you want here, Ingram?' asked Dick Binney. 'Have you come to crow over Red Moffet?'

'No,' said Ingram quietly. 'But I'd like to talk to him, if I may.'

'Go on straight down the aisle. You'll find him there.'

Down the aisle went Ingram, and behind the bars of a cell he saw, among the shadows, the form of a man, his face illumined faintly, now and then, by the red pulsation of light as he puffed at a cigarette.

'Moffet?' he asked.

'Yes. Who's that?'

'Reginald Ingram.'

'You've come over to see the finish of me, I suppose?'

'I've come over to pray for you, man,' said Ingram.

'What on earth!' cried Red Moffet. 'D'you think that I want prayers from a whining yellow mongrel of a sky pilot?'

Ingram lurched at the bars of the cell. He gripped them and hung close, breathing hard, a raging fury in his blood and brain. The man in the cell stepped closer to the bars, in turn.

'Why,' he said, 'it seems sort of irritatin', does it, when I call you by name?'

'God sustain me!' said Ingram. Then he added: 'A mob fills the street, Moffet. When they rush this place, I don't think that the sheriff and his two companions will stand very long against them. And now that you have come to this desperate time, Moffet, I want to know in what way I can serve –'

'You lie!' said Red Moffet. 'The fact is that

you've come over to enjoy the killing of me!'

Ingram sighed. But in the little pause which followed, he asked himself seriously if the prisoner were not right. For what else had drawn him to the jail with such an irresistible force? Had he felt, really, that he could be of help to Moffet? Had he felt that he could control the crowd?

He said suddenly: 'I hope that you're not right, Moffet. I hope that I've come here from a better motive.'

'That's right,' said Moffet. 'Be honest; be honest, man, and shame the hypocritical devil that's in a good many of you sky pilots.'

There was a wilder burst of noise outside, and the wave of sound crowded up around the walls of the jail. Those inside could make out the voice of a ringleader shouting; and then they heard Dick Binney defying the crowd and swearing that the prisoner would never be taken except at the cost of a dozen lives.

The minister heard Moffet groan bitterly: 'Oh, God, for a gun and a chance to die fighting! Ingram! Ingram! Find me a gun, or a club! What's the matter with me, askin' a hound of a sky pilot for help!'

Ingram retreated to the farther side of the aisle, dizzy, his head whirling with many ideas. He was trembling from head to foot – as he had trembled in the old days when he waited for the signal which would send him trotting out upon the field with the team.

There was another roar and a wave of running feet, but this time it curled around the jail and there was a sudden crash against the back door.

'The back door, Binney! Dick! Dick! *The back door*!' shouted Moffet.

He rushed to the bars and shook them with his frenzy, but Binney was already running to the back of the jail, cursing. His two assistants had had enough. They were out of the fight before it began, and Binney had to face the crowd alone.

He was within a stride of the rear door when it was beaten in, and a swarm of men, leaping through the breach, bore him down and trampled him under foot. Up the aisle of the jail they poured, their terrible masked faces illumined by the swinging light of heavy lanterns which they carried.

Then Ingram leaped into their path.

He raised both hands before them, looking gigantic in the strange, moving light.

'Friends and brothers!' he called to them. 'In the name of the Father of Mercy, I protest –'

'Get that yellow-livered fool out of the way!' called a voice, and half a dozen rude shoulders crashed against Ingram and beat him out of the path.

'A couple of you hold the sky pilot,' ordered

another voice. 'Now, gimme those keys you got from Binney!'

13
Things in General

It was dreadful to Ingram to stand pinned against the opposite range of bars, held on either side by a stalwart fellow, while the leader of the mob jangled the keys and tried them rapidly in the lock.

'He's shakin' like a leaf,' said one of Ingram's captors to the other.

'Sure,' said the second man, 'he looks real, but he ain't. He's a make-believe man. Stand fast, Ingram, or I'll bash you in the head, you big sap!'

Ingram stood still!

He heard a voice snarling at Moffet: 'Now, Red, what d'you say about yourself? The shoe's on the other foot, ain't it?'

'I know you, "Lefty",' said Red Moffet, his voice calm. 'You never heard of a time when I was part of a mob at a lynching. I've fought fair all my life, and you know it, you swine!'

'Swine, am I?' said Lefty. 'I'll have that out of your hide before you swing.'

'Shut up!' barked the leader. 'These keys don't fit. Hold on – by Heaven, I've got it!'

And the next moment the door to Red Moffet's cell swung open.

Then Reginald Oliver Ingram found his strength, as he had found it on other days when the whistle sounded the commencement of the game. The grip of those who held him slipped away from his muscles which had become like coiling serpents of steel. He thrust the men staggering back and sprang into the crowd.

A round half dozen had rushed into the little cell the instant the door was opened as the yell of the two guards rang out: 'Look out for Ingram! He's running amuck!'

The others whirled, hardly knowing what to expect, and as they whirled, Ingram plunged through them. They seemed to him shadows rather than men. He had known how to rip through a line of trained and ready athletes. He went through these unprepared cow-punchers and miners as though they had been nothing. Reaching the cell, he slammed the door with such a crash that the spring lock snapped, and the bunch of keys fell violently to the floor.

A hand reached instantly for those keys – Ingram stamped on the wrist and was answered by a scream of pain.

At the same time a pair of arms closed heavily around his body.

It would not be fair, of course, on a football field; but this was not a football field. Ingram snapped his fist home behind the ear of the assailant, and the arms which had pinned him relaxed. Others were coming at him, leaping, crowding one another so that their arms had no play; and, with his back to the cell door, which contained Moffet and his half dozen would-be lynchers, the minister stood at bay.

The nervous tension which had made him shake like a frightened child in the cold before the crisis, now enabled him to act with the speed of lightning. He struck not a single blind blow. He saw nothing but the point of the jaw, and into that charging rank he sent two blows that tore out the center of it.

Arms reached for him; a rifle whizzed past his head; but he brushed the reaching arms aside, and plucked the rifle from the hands which wielded it.

The men gave back before the sway of it with a yell of fear. Two or three lay crushed on the floor of the jail. He stepped over or on the bodies and struck savagely into the whirling mass of humanity.

The butt of the rifle struck flesh; there was a shriek of pain.

The rifle stock burst from its barrel as though it had been made of paper!

Then a gun spat fire in Ingram's face. He smote with the naked rifle barrel in the direction of that blinding flash of light, and there was a groan and a fall.

Panic seized the crowd in that narrow aisle. They had no room to use their numbers. Many of them had fallen before the onslaught of this inspired fighter. They shrank from him; he followed on their heels.

And suddenly they turned and fled, beating each other down, trampling on one another, turning and striking frantic blows at their assailant, who now seemed a giant. And half a dozen times a revolver bullet was fired at him, point-blank. Panic, however, made the hands shake that held the guns, and Ingram drove the crowd on before him, striking mercilessly with his terrible club and treading groaning men under foot as he went.

So the mob of rioters was vomited from the back door of the jail. As they swept out, two or three frightened fugitives, who had dragged themselves from the floor on which they lay stunned, staggered past Ingram and into the kindly dark.

Into that doorway Ingram stepped. He shook the broken rifle toward the mob which was swirling and pitching here and there like water.

Those behind wished to press forward; and those who had been in the jail dreaded more than death to get within the reach of that terrible churchman.

'You yelping dogs!' called Ingram in a voice of thunder. 'The door of the jail is open here. Come when you're ready! Next time I'll meet you with bullets – and I'll shoot to kill. Do you hear?'

There was a yell of rage from the crowd. Half a dozen bullets sang about Ingram's ears. He laughed at the crowd, and strode back through the doorway.

On either side of the opening he placed a lantern, of which several had been dropped by the fleeing mob. Their light would bring into sharp relief any one who tried to pass through that doorway; and it would be strange indeed if that cowed host of lynchers dared to attempt the passage.

From the cell where the foremost members of the lynching party were held safe with Red Moffet there was now rising a wild appeal for help. The men called by name upon their companions, who remained in the darkness outside. They begged and pleaded for the opening of that door which they had unlocked with such glee.

Now from the floor near the rear of the jail, a man rose up and staggered toward Ingram. It was Dick Binney, with a smear of blood on one side of his face, where he had been struck by the butt of a heavy Colt. He had a gun in either hand, and his lips were twitching. Ingram felt that he never before had seen a man so ready for desperate needs.

'Ingram,' he said, 'God bless you for givin' me another chance at 'em! Oh, the scoundrels! I'm gunna make 'em pay for this! I'm gunna make 'em pay!'

There was a litter of weapons on the floor of the aisle, where five men lay, either unconscious or writhing in terrible pain.

The sheriff and Ingram gathered the fallen and placed them in a corner, while the sheriff's two assistants now again appeared and offered to guard the prisoners. Their proffer of help was accepted in scornful silence, and the sheriff went back to the main prize of the evening – the half dozen ringleaders who were cooped safely in Red Moffet's cell.

Then a strange thing happened.

For the six were well armed – armed to the teeth in fact – and yet they had not the slightest thought of resistance. They crowded against the bars and with piteous voices begged the sheriff to let them out. They promised, like repentant children, that they would be good hereafter. They vowed to the deputy sheriff eternal gratitude.

Dick Binney, his face stiff with congealed blood, grinned sourly as he listened. Then he opened the door and permitted them to come out, one by one. At the cell door they were relieved of their weapons, and held in check by Reginald Ingram. They were before him like sheep before a shepherd. For the Reverend Reginald Ingram was a much altered man.

A random bullet had chipped his ear, and sprinkled him with streaks of blood. His coat had been torn from his back. One sleeve of his shirt was rent away, exposing a bare arm on which the iron muscles were piled and coiled. And perhaps his chief decoration was a great swelling – already blue-black – which closed one eye to a narrow, evil squint.

This terrible giant herded the prisoners along the bars, the bent barrel of the rifle, more terrible by far than any loaded gun, still in his hand. He spoke to the crestfallen men with a cheerful contempt. They would be held for attempted murder, and they would be treated as cowards should be treated. He ripped the masks from their faces, and called them by their names. And they shrank and trembled before him.

When the sheriff had emptied Red Moffet's cell, he locked up the recent aggressors, one by one, in adjoining cells. A miserable row they made! With them went three of the stunned men whom Ingram had trampled in the aisle. Two others of his victims were better suited for the hospital than the jail, and Binney's assistants cared for them in the office as well as they could.

Outside, the noise of the crowd had ceased with mysterious suddenness. When Binney cast a glance through the open rear door, half suspecting that his enemies might have massed covertly for a sudden thrust, there was not a soul in sight. Apparently, on reflection, the crowd had decided that there had been enough done that night – or enough attempted! They had remembered other employments. They had scattered swiftly and silently.

A cell door had clicked shut for the ninth time, and nine men were cursing or groaning behind bars, when a hand was clapped on the bare shoulder of the minister. He turned and confronted Red Moffet, whose face was transformed by a magnificent grin of triumph.

'Old-timer,' said Red Moffet, 'of all the good turns that was ever done for me, the best –'

He was silenced by a lionlike roar from the minister.

'Moffet, what are you doing out of your cell? Get back inside it!'

'Me?' said Moffet, blinking, and then he added:

'Look here, Ingram, you've been playin' dog to a lot of sheep, but that don't mean that you can –'

'Get back in that cell, you – you puppy!' ordered Ingram.

'I'll see you there first!' began Red Moffet.

Feeling that words were not apt to have much effect upon this bloodstained, ragged monster, Red followed his speech with a long, driving, overhand right which was aimed full at the point of Ingram's jaw.

It was an honest, whole-hearted punch, famous in many a town and cow camp throughout the Western range. It was sure death, sudden darkness, and a long sleep when it landed. But this time it somehow failed to land. The minister's head dropped a little to one side, and Moffet's thick arm drove over his shoulder; then, while Red rushed on into a clinch, Ingram swung his right fist up from his knee, swung it up, and rose on his toes with the sway of it, and put the full leverage of his straightening back into the blow.

It struck Red Moffet just beneath the chin and caused his feet to leave the floor and the back of his head to fall heavily between his shoulder blades. When his feet came down again, there was no strength in his knees to support his weight. A curtain of darkness had fallen over his brain. He dropped headlong into the arms of Ingram.

Those arms picked him up and carried him into

his cell, laid him carefully on his cot, and folded his arms upon his chest.

'You didn't kill him, Ingram?' asked the overawed sheriff, peering through the bars as Ingram came out of the cell and slammed the door.

'No,' said Ingram. 'He'll be all right in a few minutes. And,' he added, looking around him, 'I hope that everything will be quiet here now, Binney?'

'Partner,' grinned Dick Binney, 'nobody could start trouble in this town for a month – after what you've done to-night! And – suppose we shake hands on things in general?'

They shook hands on things in general.

14

Muy Diablo, After All

It would be impossible to describe all that passed through the mind of the Reverend Reginald Ingram when he released the hand of the deputy sheriff. For, with a shock, he was recalled to himself. And he realized that, no matter how else his conduct might be described, it certainly had been most unministerial!

He did not have time to reflect upon the matter in any detail, nor to decide how he could reconcile what his fists had done with certain prescriptions in the Gospels. For now there was a violent interruption on his train of thought. Horses were heard galloping up the street. They stopped near the jail.

'It's more trouble! Stand by me, Ingram!' cried the deputy sheriff, picking up a repeating rifle. 'If they try to rush that door open, I'm going to blow a few of them sky high! These are some of the friends of the boys in the cells, yonder! Ingram, will you stand by me?'

'I will,' said the minister. And, automatically, he reached for a weapon from the sheriff's stock. It was a great, ponderous, old-fashioned, double-barreled shotgun, loaded with buckshot, adequate to blow a whole column of charging men back through yonder doorway.

Voices were heard calling, crying back and forth. Then into the bright lantern light which flooded the doorway, a figure sprang. Ingram tilted his weapon –

'No!' cried the deputy sheriff.

And he struck up the muzzles of the shotgun just as the triggers were pulled, and a double charge blasted its way through the flimsy roofing and on toward the stars.

'It's a woman!' called Dick Binney.

Aye, it was a woman who ran toward them now, crying: 'Dick Binney! Dick Binney! Where's Reggie Ingram? What've you done with him?'

Astrid was as unconcerned as though a popgun had been fired at her. Behind, charging through the doorway, came Vasa and a few of his neighbors to protect the girl. She disregarded them utterly. She found Dick Binney and caught hold of his rifle.

'Dick! – Dick! You've let the brutes murder Reggie, and I'll –'

'Hey, quit it, will you?' exclaimed Dick Binney, striving vainly to free his gun – for he was not quite sure of the intentions of the cavalcade which clattered up the aisle of the jail. 'I didn't touch Reggie, as you call him. Here he is to speak for himself.'

The girl looked across at the tattered giant; and at the second glance she was able to recognize him.

'Reggie!' she screamed.

And all at once Ingram was enveloped – subdued – dragged forward beneath the light – kissed – wept over – exclaimed about – it would be impossible to express all the storm of joy and grief and fury which burst from Astrid Vasa.

It appeared that the large minister was an innocent darling, and all other men were beasts and wolves; and it further appeared that he was a blessed lamb, and that his Astrid loved him more than heaven and earth joined together; moreover, the man who had made his eye so black was simply hateful, and she would never speak to that man again –

'But, oh, Reggie,' she breathed at last, 'didn't you just have a gorgeous, glorious, ripping, everlasting good time out of it?'

He hesitated. He blinked. The question touched exactly the center of his odd reflections.

'Yes,' he said faintly and sadly. 'I'm afraid that that is exactly what I have been having. And,' he added, 'I'm frightfully depressed, Astrid. I've disgraced myself and my profession and my –'

The rest of the sentence was lost. Astrid was hugging him with the vehement delight of a child.

She dragged him forth. She pointed with pride to his tatters and to his wounds.

'Look!' cried she. 'Look at him! And he's ashamed! Oh, was there ever such a wonderful, silly, dear, foolish, good-for-nothing in the world?'

They got Ingram out of the jail.

The town was up by the time they reached the street. It had not been very safe to venture abroad during the period when the would-be lynching party had possession of the streets, but now it was perfectly safe, and, therefore, all hands had turned out and were raising a great commotion. And in the forefront, nearest to the jail, were the families of sundry gentlemen who, it was rumored, were now fast confined within its walls. And Heaven knew what would become of them when the law had had its way!

Ingram appeared, disfigured, vastly unministerial, with Astrid Vasa at his side, and a small corps of men, heavily armed, walking behind the couple.

The crowd gave way.

'Brother Pedrillo was right, after all,' said a bystander. 'This feller sure is *muy diablo*.'

'*Muy diablo*!' murmured Astrid, looking fondly up at her hero. 'Do you hear what they're saying about you?'

'Ah, my dear,' said the battered hero. 'I hear it, and I'm afraid it shows me that I have done my last work for the church.'

'Bah!' said Astrid. 'You can do better work now than you've ever done before. You can build hospitals over the whole face of the country, if you have a mind to. By Jiminy, I'll make dad give you the money for another one right away, if you'll have it!

The minister made no reply.

He was too busy thinking of various widely disjointed phases of this business, and most of all he was wondering what sort of report would go back to the reverend council which had dispatched him to this far mission in the West?

He said good night to Astrid at her house, and went on up the street toward his own little shack. And as he came the crowd – which was returning from the region of the jail, where they had been picking up the detailed story of the fight – gave way around him, and let him have a clean pathway. He had been downtrodden, cheaper than dirt in their eyes. He was something else, now. He moved among them like a Norse god, a figure only dimly conceived in the midst of winter storm and mist. So Reginald Oliver Ingram walked down the main street of Billman and entered his shack.

As he entered, the strong odor of cigar smoke rolled out toward him. He lighted the lantern, and saw Brother Pedrillo seated in his one comfortable chair, smiling broadly at him.

'These cigars of yours,' said Brother Pedrillo, 'are very good. And I thought that, after all, you probably owed me one, being *muy diablo*, as it appears you are!'

There was a change in the church affairs of Billman. Indeed, for the first time in the history of the town, the activities of the church had to do with something more than weddings and funerals. Men who were a little past the first flush of wild youth formed the habit of drifting into the church on Sundays. Because, for one thing, all the other best men in the community were fairly sure to be there. They came for the sake of talking business after the church session had ended.

But then they began to grow a little more enthusiastic about the church itself. The manner of the young minister was not that of one speaking from a cloud. He spoke calmly and earnestly about such matters of the heart and soul as interest all men, and with such a conversational air that sometimes his rhetorical questions actually drew forth answers from his congregation. No one could ever have called it an intense congregation, or one that took its religion with a poisonous seriousness. But, before the winter came, it was a congregation which supported two schools and a hospital. It acquired a mayor and a legal system that worked as smoothly as the system in any Eastern city. And it was noted with a good deal of interest that in the political campaigns there was one speaker who was always upon the winning side, and he was none other than the gentleman of the clerical collar – young Reginald Oliver Ingram.

'How come?' asked a stranger from Nevada. 'Might it be because he's got such a pretty wife, maybe, that he's got such a powerful lot of influence with people?'

'I'll tell you the real reason of it,' replied a townsman, drawing the Nevada man aside. 'You take another look. Now, what d'you see?'

'I see a big sap of a sky pilot.'

'Stranger, I'm an old man. But don't speak like that to one of the younger boys of the town, or they'll knock your head off. I'll tell you the real reason why Ingram runs this town. It ain't just because he's a parson. It's because he's *muy diablo*, and we all know it!'

VALLEY OF JEWELS

I

Behind the Dust Cloud

It was so hot that nobody in Cherryville had the ambition to stand up and look to see what caused the dust cloud that was rolling toward us down the road. When that dust cloud dragged closer, we could see the nodding heads of a pair of mules, in the lead team; and, pretty soon, somebody said that it must be 'Buck' Logan's mules.

That was right. It was Buck, and he brought the queerest load from the railroad that we had ever dreamed about. A load of lumber!

He pulled up at the wátering trough; and he slipped the checks of his eight mules; and he let them have a drink. And while they were drinking, the steaming smell of melting pitch came rolling from the heaped and shining lumber on that big wagon and stung our nostrils.

'Buck,' said some one, 'who might the lucky party be that's to get that lumber?'

Buck looked up and shifted his quid; but, when the lump was settled in his other cheek, he changed his mind about answering and started checking up his mules again, pulling their heads hard to get them away from the water. Even a mule, which is too mean to be hurt by hardly anything, is a lot better off without too much cold water after a long pull.

Then Logan climbed up to his seat and called to his team; but, when they hit the collars, a mule in the swing span came back as if from a sore shoulder – and the load wasn't started.

We forgot about our question. We were all too busy calling advice and laughing at Buck and enjoying the show.

Buck got into a towering rage. He was right proud of that mule team. They had cost him a good deal of money and care. He'd been here and he'd been there, getting sizes and colors that matched, and now he had a perfect set. They were all of the same gray shade to a hair. They tapered from big, sixteen-hand wheelers to mean, jack-rabbity-looking leaders, faster and smarter than you would believe. That team could pull a mountain of lead!

However, the watering trough had been overflowing; and the ground was streaked with mud, into which one of the forewheels had worked down. So Buck had a time giving his team a hitch to the left and then a hitch to the right, and trying to break that wheel out of the mud and get the wagon rolling.

It was a big load, and a couple of those mules were sore-shouldered. Even the best care in the world couldn't keep a mule or a horse from having its shoulders knocked up if they worked those rough mountain roads.

By this time nobody had any foolish idea that Buck would waste time answering questions about where that load of fine lumber was going. He was simply white with rage, to be shamed by his team in front of so many folks.

And of course we made him feel it. A hardy fellow like Buck, with a vanity about mules, couldn't be turned loose without feeling the whip. If he laid the lash on his team, we laid the lash on Buck.

We even managed to stand up to do it.

Says Rod Gruger, 'It's a shame how a mule team will run downhill. That was a likely enough team about six months back. And now look at them; they can't pull a paper weight off of a greased skid.'

He said this sympathetic and shaking his head, and he went on, 'If Buck was a fellow who would take advice, it's about time that somebody should up and tell him that a mule team like that is worth good care and good food. You can't give 'em thistledown for fodder and expect them to get fat. What about it, boys?'

We agreed in a chorus, I can tell you. And Buck, he pretended not to hear; but all the time his neck kept getting redder and redder, and all the time he was getting a straighter set on his mouth. Every now and then he cursed us out of the corners of his eyes. He was a hardy-looking fellow, Buck Logan. I never seen a two-handed fighter that looked more of the part than Buck did.

But what nearly drove him mad now was the knowledge that there was nothing that human care could give to those mules that they didn't get from him. He never worked them too hard; and he was always slaving at their harness, or going out of his way to haul in supplies of crushed barley for them. And he could have made twice as much money out of them, if he had only been willing to treat them like mules and not like babies.

However, we had our good time with him.

I jumped down and got my roan horse, Jupe, and led him around in front of the big mule team. He was about as big as a minute, though he was the hardiest little jack rabbit that ever bucked off a saddle or followed a calf like a snake through a herd.

'Hey, Buck,' says I, 'just pass me out that extra fifth chain that you got under your wagon, and I'll pull you out with Jupe, here!'

That was more than Buck could stand. He threw down his blacksnake, and he yanked the four-horse whip out of the socket and came for me.

I barely had enough time to climb into the saddle before the lash of that whip screamed past my ear. It would almost of cut my head off if it had hit me; but I got away, with a yell, old Jupe nearly jumping out of his skin to get from the path of that whip.

Buck threw his hat down in the dust and stamped on it, he was so mad; and the boys on the veranda nearly died. They simply hung onto one another and cried, they had to laugh so hard. But after a while Buck went around to his mules, and he said something at the head of each one of them and gave them a slap on the neck.

It was a wonderful thing to see him take them in hand. They had been getting more and more restless, listening to the yelling and the foolishness of that gang of cow-punchers on the porch; but Buck quieted them down, and then he went back and jumped up on the back of his near wheeler and laid his hand on the jerk line.

You could fairly see every ear in that procession of mules tip back to listen to the voice of the boss. Buck yelled, and that near leader stepped forward and took up the slack in the fifth chain, and the rest of the mules leaned just enough into the collars to get the kinks out. Then the blacksnake cut the air and cracked, and Buck yelled again.

Well, it was a pretty sight. Some people can't see anything in horseflesh except the racers with their long pedigrees and their fancy ways; but I've always seen a good deal in a work horse. They're an honest lot, you know. And work mules come right next for my admiration.

Those eight mules leaned into their collars. They scratched like dogs until they worked their way through that surface dust and got down to a firm footing; but, when their little hoofs held, they just stiffened their legs and hung in the collars, with the hips sinking down, and the harness standing high up above their backs.

It did a man good to watch them. And that wagon lurched, staggered, and then got out of the rut – and there was the mule team breaking into a trot to keep the wagon from running over them.

We liked Buck in spite of the queer ways he had, and we couldn't help giving him a cheer when he got his heavy wagon out as slick as all that.

In the meantime, a dozen of us slid onto our horses and followed down the road to see where in the town he was going to leave that lumber.

But he didn't stop. He went right on through Cherryville and pointed the heads of those horses for the big rough mountains, where there was never a sign of a town within a good hundred miles.

II

A Fight in the Offing

Some of us thought that Buck must be mad; some of the rest thought that there might have been a new purchase of land in the last few weeks, and that this lumber was meant for building a new house. When we asked the sheriff – and he knew everything of importance that happened in the country – he said that there had been no sale. So where could Buck Logan have gone with that wagon?

We wished afterward that we had followed him right on. But a whole week went by before he hove through Cherryville bound in the same direction, and with another load of lumber. It was dusk of the day, however; and there was nothing for Buck but to put up at the hotel.

We buzzed all around his team and his wagon while he was putting it up; and we tried everything but questions, because we knew that Buck was one of the most silent men in the world. But nothing came out of what we could see. At supper Buck sat down in the corner seat at the table – I mean, he sat in the chair that was always for me, which will be explained as I go along.

Anyway, when I came in and saw Buck seated in that chair, the boys all grinned at me, very broad and very expectant. They thought that I would tackle Buck and tell him to get out of that chair. But that wasn't my style. I've never liked fighting. And if trouble has sat down beside me more than once in my life, it hasn't been because I've invited it. I didn't like to be away from my usual place, but I thought that I could stand it for one night. So I took a chair as near the other corner as I could. By hitching my chair around to the side a good deal, I could keep my eye on the two doors that opened into the room, and there was only one window that bothered me. It opened behind my shoulder, and every minute it was like a gun pointed at my back.

However, I was willing to accept that misery even if it gave me indigestion. It was better to me than hunting for a fight with Buck Logan. And nobody could expect to get that big Logan out of a chair without a fight.

Nothing would have come out of this, if it hadn't been that the boys couldn't keep their mouths shut. They had to start talking. And about the first thing they whispered was loud enough to fetch down the table to my ears, and therefore I knew that it must have got to the ears of Logan, too.

Said some fool among the boys: 'It'll happen after the supper is over. "Doc" Willis will rip into Logan then and tear him to bits.'

I could have murdered the boy who whispered that. I didn't dare to look down the table, and yet from the corner of my eye I could see Buck Logan lifting his head like a lion and glaring at me. Altogether, it was what I'd call a mean situation. I've known killings to start with a lot less. A whole lot less!

But that was not all that happened, and that was not all that was said. There was a buzz and a murmuring on all the time. Most of it was for the benefit of Buck.

I finished my meal as fast as I could and got out on the veranda and wedged myself against the wall. But still it was a long time before the little chills stopped wriggling up and down my back. I finished my first cigarette; and then a couple of the boys came out, and big Buck Logan was at their heels. He rambled straight up to me and he sings out for me and the world to hear:

'Say, kid, I understand that you're gunna eat me. Eat me raw and swaller me right down. Lemme hear what you think about it?'

He was plumb offensive, I must say; but I knew that the boys had been working Buck up to this point. He was a big man and a mean man in a silent sort of a way – which is the meanest of all – but he was not the sort of a fellow to hunt trouble. He had enough of that with his mules. So I looked him over and swallowed the first half dozen answers that jumped up to the tip of my tongue.

I merely said, 'Logan, I think the boys have been talking a lot of bunk to you. I don't want any trouble with you. Not a bit! Sit down and make yourself at home.'

I pointed to the chair beside me and smiled at him. Nothing could have been more friendly than that, though I admit that it may have given him a pretty good excuse for thinking the thought that I saw in his face.

He simply wrinkled up with contempt and with disgust, and he turned around on his heel and strode off toward the barn.

I sat there rubbing my cheek, because I felt exactly as though I had been hit in the face. And I heard one of the lads break out:

'By the heavens, Doc is going to take it!'

And somebody else said, 'Logan looks pretty big to him.'

That lifted me right out of my chair, but after an instant I made myself settle down again. They could say what they pleased. The day had been – and not so very long before – when a pair of speeches like this would have made me go gunning for the biggest man in the world, with my teeth set. But I had had a good deal of the foolishness knocked out of me, and my nerves were a long distance from being what they had once been.

I had been insulted. There was no doubt of that. Whan a man refuses to answer a decent question and turns on his heel and walks away, it's enough insult to satisfy anybody, I suppose. But at the same time I couldn't help wanting to dodge the trouble if it were possible.

You see, Buck Logan was a square fellow, from what I'd seen and heard of him. At least, I'd seen him handle a mule team in a pinch without any brutality; and that was more than I could say about any other mule skinner I can recall. No, I felt that Buck Logan was a good fellow and that it would pay me a lot to avoid the bad side of him. As for these other fellows, let them say what they wanted to about me. Words are not ounce bullets. Not by a lot they aren't!

I made me another cigarette and lighted it and snapped the match off into the darkness. I felt that I was as cool and as calm as could be, but I was wrong. I was all brittle and ready to break, and it only took a snap of the fingers to do it.

Matter of fact, I'm ashamed to tell what set me off. But a grizzly old cat that belonged in the hotel came sauntering down the porch, and I wanted to show how easy and careless I was by pretending not to notice the eyes that were on me and the smiles and the wonder and the contempt that was showing on their faces. But when I reached out my hand and talked soft to the cat, it arched its back and spat at me, and then it jumped off the veranda into the night.

That brought a roar of laughter. I don't know why. But it sent a rush of red-hot blood spinning into my brain. I jumped up from my chair and walked over where the rest of the boys were.

'Are you laughing at me?' said I.

That sobered them. But even when they were silent, I was still raging.

'I asked you if you was laughing at me, by any chance. Do I hear you answer?'

Then somebody lost in the shadows in the rear drawled: 'You better ask Buck Logan about that.'

I yelled, 'Curse Buck Logan! Some of you go tell him that I say he's a rat; and that if he don't come here to me I'll come to find him; and there ain't any hole deep enough to hide him from me.'

Then I began to walk up and down that veranda, hotter than ever. But I wasn't so angry that I didn't notice two or three of the boys detach themselves and wander off toward the barn. So I knew that Logan would hear what I had said, and hear it with trimmings, too. And I knew that that was apt to make for a gun fight – the very thing that I had dodged safely for two whole years, and that I had vowed I would never go through with again. However, a man can't change his nature. I was raised too much around guns. And I had spent too many years in Mexico – a wild and bad place, believe me.

After a little time I heard footsteps coming, and in the lead there was a long, heavy stride that I figured must be Buck Logan. Yes, here he came, right up the steps out of the night, and stood there under the gasoline lamp.

I said to myself that he was as good as a dead man, that minute. I was full of concentrated poison, and full of concentrated coldness, too. What happens in moments like that are a blur to some people; a blur to most honest men. I suppose – but not to me. when the devil takes me by the throat he multiplies me by ten, and I felt the strength of ten in me at that moment.

I saw Buck Logan as complete as though he were painted by my hand in oils. I saw his faded blue shirt, and the wrinkles in his overalls around the knees, and the hard knot of his bandanna around his neck, and the sunstained felt hat on his head. I saw the low, handy fit of the Colt at his right hip, too; and I looked through his pale-blue eyes into his soul and thought that he was as brave and as stern a man as I had ever seen in my life – but that made no difference. I was set for a kill, and I looked on Logan as a man living but already more than half dead.

He looked me over, too. He was just as calm as me, but there was no fire in his eyes. His hands were his best weapons, and not his guns; I could tell that, I thought.

Then he said, 'Willis, I hear that you've been saying hard things about me.'

'I'll say them over again, if you want to hear them,' said I.

'I don't want to hear them,' said Logan. 'If I do hear them, I'll have to fight you. And I'm not ready to start pushing the daisies.'

III

A Try-Out

Well, take the time and the place and the rest into consideration, and you'll have to admit that that was a good deal of a speech for a man to make. But though those boys who stood around and watched were a hardy gang as ever stepped, not one of them smiled and not one of them made the mistake of thinking that Buck was taking water.

I didn't make that mistake, either. I sat down again in my chair.

I said, 'Buck, the trouble was that you made a mite of a mistake about me; but I never made any mistake about you. I don't want any trouble with you if I can avoid it. I feel plumb friendly to you, if you'll give me a chance to act that way.'

'Friend,' says Buck Logan, 'is a word that I don't use more than once every ten years; but maybe I could make an exception this evening. We'll shake hands, if you say the word.'

Yes, we did shake hands, and when those big bony fingers of his closed over mine they made me feel as weak as a baby. He sat down and turned his big head toward the others.

'Scatter, kids,' said he. 'This here is a time for man talk, and you're too young to listen.'

They didn't wait to be invited twice. They just faded away here and there, and we were left alone.

'It was the little roan hoss,' said Buck, after a time.

I nodded.

'Here's the makings,' said I; 'smoke up.'

He shook his head and pulled out a black pipe. Then he whittled some shavings off of a black plug, and filled his bowl with that stuff; and when he lighted up, a cloud of smoke that would of killed mosquitoes filled the air. There was no doubt about Buck being a mansized man. One whiff of that pipe smoke of his was enough to settle the question. It made me fair dizzy.

'It was the roan,' said Buck again.

'Sure,' said I, and nodded again. 'I understand.'

About ten minutes later he added, 'My mules is close to me, Willis.'

'Sure,' said I. 'I understand.'

And, about half an hour later he said, 'Time for me to turn in. This here was a fine talk, Willis.'

And he went off to bed.

You can count the words that had gone to the making of that 'fine talk'. But I felt that I knew Buck, and he felt that he knew me.

I turned out at the first crack of day, because I've ridden the range so long that the sun doesn't let me sleep late; and, when I came down, there were the mules all strung out in front of the load of lumber, and Buck hitching them in their places. He must have got up an hour before the light began, because he had that whole team fed and harnessed and curried down as slick as a whistle.

I stepped out and gave him a hand till he warned me to stop.

'They know their boss,' said Buck Logan; 'but with strangers, they think that they're tigers and that they can live on raw meat. Mind the heels of that gray devil on the off point.'

I side-stepped just as the heels of the off-pointer whistled past my ear.

Buck Logan stepped back to his place and took hold on the jerk line.

'Look here, Doc,' said he, 'what's your job?'

'I still got most of a month's wages to blow in,' said I.

'How come?'

'Poker has been good to me.'

'Poker,' says he, and grins; 'and then what?'

'I got the best cutting hoss on the range,' said I. 'I'll pick me up a job, when that money is blowed in!'

'Fine,' says he. 'Riding range?'

'Riding herd, I suppose.'

'How about man-sized work, Doc?'

'I dunno what you mean.'

'Real pay.'

'What kind?'

'Fifty a week.'

I whistled. 'That's better than ten,' said I.

'Does it sound to you?'

'Not a bit.'

'Why not? Like poker better?'

'No, poker always licks me in the end.'

'Well?'

'I'm not a fifty-dollar-a-week man, Buck. Fifty a month is more to my style.'

'No chances, eh?'

'Buck,' said I, 'how old am I?'

'Thirty-two,' says he, quick as a wink.

'You miss me by seven years,' I told him.

'You're not thirty-nine,' said he.

'I'm not.'

'The devil!' said Buck. 'Are you only a kid of twenty-five?'

'I'm twenty-five,' said I; 'but I'm not a kid.'

'You wear your gray hair right along with me,' said he. 'And you ain't got the fool look.'

'I've had the foolishness shot out of me,' said I.

He nodded. 'I had a pal fifteen years ago that was that way. Quietest man that ever lived; but he was like you, one of these here lion tamers.'

'Go easy, partner,' said I.

'I'm not kidding you,' said Buck Logan. 'If you've been shot up so much that seven years have leaked out with the blood – why, I'm not fool enough to talk down to you. Only this job I'd—'

'I ain't tempted,' said I.

'Why not?'

'I hate fighting.'

'I didn't say that.'

'No, but I guess that. Fifty a week in these days means one of two things – crooked work or guns. Well, you're not a crook, Buck.'

'Thanks,' said he. 'But fifty a week is fifty a week.'

'It depends on how long the weeks last.'

'I know, but this job is different. It ain't dangerous, but it may be. You better saddle your hoss and come along.'

'I have swore off on being a fool,' said I.

'Swear on again,' said Buck; 'you're too young to miss the fun.'

'Buck,' said I, 'it's fine of you; but it won't do. I'd like to be with you, but I won't go.'

He only grinned. 'I've planted the poison in you,' said Buck. 'I'm taking the Creek road, and I'll expect you to catch up with me by noon. So long till then, kid.'

He hollered to his mules. They hit their collars with a snap, and the big wagon with its shining load of white lumber rolled on down the road.

I turned my back on it after I had watched it out of sight, but when I walked back to the hotel I heard a rumbling of distant thunder and turned around with a start. I could see nothing, but I knew that that was the big wagon crossing the bridge and turning onto the Creek road.

Who the devil would want to cart good lumber like that up the Creek road? I had thought that Buck was joking when he told me that; but now I knew for certain that he had meant what he said, and the mystery of the thing began to work on me like wine in the blood.

Well, I turned my shoulder on the temptation as firmly as I could; and I went about the morning calmly enough. After breakfast I sat in at a three-handed game, and about ten in the morning I had a hundred and fifty dollars stacked upon the table in front of me. I was in the middle of the neatest winning streak that I had ever started. The cards were for me. There was plenty of coin in that party, and I felt that I could drift my way to a year's holiday by noon.

But all at once I had to jump up from my chair and push all my winnings back into the game.

'Boys,' said I, 'there's your cash. I can't sit this game out, and I won't quit while you still want revenge. So long!'

They stared at me as though they thought that I was a madman; but I ran on up to my room, jerked my things together, and hurried out to the barn.

In five minutes more I was running Jupe up the trail. We came to the old Creek bridge – looking so rickety that I wondered how it could ever have stood the weight of the big wagon and its heavy load – but there was the track of the wheels, down the middle of it, and the great steel tires had sunk half an inch deep into the rotten surface.

I put Jupe at a hard run across that bridge and fanned him over the next hill with my quirt. After that I settled back in the saddle and took things easy, because I knew that I had committed myself so far on this expedition that I would not turn back.

It was later than noon before I sighted the dust cloud, however; for that team of mules knew how to step out on the road, and they could do four miles an hour when they had a fair chance. At least, so big Buck claimed for them; and I believe that he was right. They were the outwalkingest mules I ever saw.

But once I had the dust in sight, I was soon up with them. Buck turned around and gave me one dusty grin. Then he trudged on beside the wagon, and I jogged along behind.

I wasn't exactly contented. I felt that there was danger and bad danger ahead of us, some place. But I still couldn't figure what that danger might be.

'Hello!' says Buck suddenly. 'Look at that buzzard, there, just out of rifle range. Queer how much sense them birds has, old-timer, eh? Know to ten yards just how far a rifle bullet will carry.'

I looked up and spotted that buzzard. It was wheeling pretty low down, as buzzards fly.

'I dunno,' said I. 'Looks to me that a bullet would fan the feathers out of that piece of misery.'

'Humph!' said Buck.

'Well,' said I, 'I'll show you, if you got any doubts.'

I pulled my Winchester out of its sheath. It was a good gun. Any Winchester is a sweet rifle; but this was extra tight and handy, and it shot as straight as a ruled line – or straighter when you got to know its habits. I tipped up the barrel, studied the flight of the buzzard, and followed it for a couple of seconds.

'Hurry up!' said Buck. 'It's climbing!'

It was climbing, well enough. You couldn't see a beat of the wings, but all at once that buzzard began to whirl around in its circle three times as fast as it had gone before. It was climbing fast, in the mysterious way that buzzards know. They may be things of horror to look at close up, but they're certainly things of wonder on the wing. And this black bit of mystery was fairly sliding off up into the heart of the sky. It was a long shot; but I got a good bead, and a pretty fair sense of the drift of the bird. Then I pulled the trigger.

'You see!' called Buck. 'Out of range!'

'If I didn't hit that bird, I'm a liar,' said I.

And just then the buzzard stopped sailing along and tumbled fast for the ground. It hit with a thump fifty yards away, but neither of us had any curiosity about taking a closer look at it.

Then I looked aside at Buck Logan; and I saw that he was trying to look calm, but that he was really swallowing a lot of exultation. His face had the look of a man who says, 'I told you so.'

Even if I had not smelled a rat long before, one glance at that expression of Logan's would have been enough to convince me that we were bound for a place where there would be a premium on straight shooting and quick thinking. He was very pleased that I had brought that buzzard down, and I could see that the old rascal had been merely trying me out without asking me to show what I could do.

IV

Daggett Valley

It was about a day after this, that we turned to the left and headed through the hills over a road where the wheels sank deep and where the wagon stalled every couple of miles and the mules had to fight and struggle to get it rolling again.

I watched the course that we were taking, and all at once I yelled at Buck:

'We're heading for the Creek! We're going right straight for Daggett Creek!'

'Son,' said he, 'you talk sense; but why for shouldn't we be heading for Daggett Creek?'

'Why for shouldn't we? Why for should we, would be a lot more reasonable question to ask, I should say. Who would want to haul lumber to Daggett Creek – unless they're going to start up with a dude ranch there?'

'Son,' said Buck, 'you can keep on guessing until the time comes – which I hope that it will come to you easy, and not in a hard lump.'

That was all he would say. But there we were, aimed across the white hills of the desert plumb in the direction of the Creek.

I said to Buck, 'Tell me the truth. Some sucker thinks that he can strike gold there again!'

'Maybe he does and maybe he doesn't,' said Buck.

'Leastwise,' said I, 'since I've rode this far into the deal with you, I think that you might open up and tell me what's what so far as you know.'

'Kid,' said Buck, 'there's nothing I appreciate more than the way that you've kept yourself from pestering me with questions on this here trip. I thought that my tongue would ache just from saying, I don't know. But you've kept your face shut. Now I'll tell you why I ain't talked out more free and easy to you – and the reason is that although you're my pal, I've given my word that I won't talk no more than I have to.'

'They've made you swear to keep things as dark as possible?'

'That's what they've done, though they must of knowed that they was taking a chance.'

'They was,' said I, 'seeing that your wagon ain't any ghost wagon. If a blind man wanted to follow you, he would have an easy time of it.'

'He would,' said Buck; 'but he would have to take along provisions for several days, I guess.'

That was true, too. The best way to discourage anybody that started on that trail would just be to let him taste some of the length of the miles and the length of the hot days.

How the mules got through it I can't guess. I know that my Jupe hoss, which was about as tough as they come in any country, was fagged and almost done for. But those mules had grain twice a day from the sacks that big Buck Logan carried along with him. And every time he came to a suspicion of a run of water, Buck would stop the team and drench them down – sloshing the water over them for an hour at a time, because he said that that done them a lot of good.

He made three halts a day – in the mid-morning – a long one at noon – and another in the middle of the long afternoon. And Heaven knows how long a hot afternoon can be in the desert! Every time he halted he would strip every peg and strap of harness from the mules, and he would wash off the sweat from their shoulders and the backs of their necks where the heavy collars galled them; and then he would turn them loose to graze on whatever grass that they could find and to enjoy a roll and a mite of freedom, at least.

Of course it took a lot of time, and it cost him more work than you would ever guess, because he had to do it all himself. Those mules didn't appreciate the touch of any human being other than Buck, and I think he was proud of having such a string of man-eaters and wanted to keep them just that way.

But the way they ate up the miles, and the way

they snaked that heavily loaded wagon through the drift sands was a caution. Half a dozen times we had to get out and shovel out trenches through the loose surface and down to the hard footing for them. But every other time they worked their own way out in a very scientific fashion.

They got thin; but they stuck to their jobs, and they were still in amazing good shape when the gray head of the leader turned through the little pass between the hills and we saw the green of the valley beneath us – Daggett Valley – and it never could have looked better, even to the gold rushers, than it did to us.

There was a boundary which you could cross in three steps, most of the way. On one side of the hills everything was dead and burned. And on the other side the sand hills showed you what they would grow when they had a fair chance to get a drink of water now and then; so that it was a pretty sight, I can tell you, with the grass growing as thick and as even and as crowded as though it had been planted.

Buck couldn't resist the temptation. He unharnessed his team right there; and we watched them break into those green fields and eat and eat, and then stop to roll, and then get up and eat again like gluttons. You couldn't of trusted a dry-fed horse with such fodder; he would of killed himself, sure. But a mule is different; it is too mean to do itself any real harm. Well, those mules feasted themselves full; and we sat down and drank in the beauty of the valley, and I'll tell you how soft we were. When a fat young buck stepped out of the brush to watch the mules playing with one another, neither Buck Logan nor myself reached for a rifle. We just felt plumb peaceful.

And, for that minute, I forgot that I was riding into danger of some kind about which I knew nothing, as yet. However, things that begin well don't always have the best endings.

V

On Guard

We didn't make any effort to forge ahead again that day. We rested, and the horse and mules rested. Bright and early the next morning, we started down the valley.

The sun was burning hot, but the minute we got among the trees everything was cool and pleasant. I never saw finer pines in my life.

We pushed up the old road which followed along beside the creek. I think we went about a mile when we heard the clinking of hammers very busy ahead of us; and, when the mules were given a halt and a breathing space, the trees were filled with echoes flying about as the hammers chattered away. It was almost like the noises that you wake up and hear in a town. I looked at Buck Logan.

However, he didn't choose to talk, and I wouldn't ask questions; but I knew that that was our goal – that place where men were busy building. And I was glad of it. There was something cheerful about the sound; it did you good to listen to it.

Then we started ahead again, and we came out from under the shadows of the big pines and into a clear stretch with only a scattering of trees here and there; and on a hillside near the creek was not a camp being built, but a big house.

It was a good, strong-built house, big enough to have maybe a dozen rooms in it; and I could guess that it must have been run up back in the days of the mining boom, when perhaps the creek looked good enough to one of the miners to be home all the year around.

Indeed, I think that some of those miners thought that the pay dirt would never give out. They got so many quick millions out of the surface dirt that they thought there had to be a continuation down into the rocks. It was too good to finish off with nothing – but, strangely, that was exactly what happened.

The gold was gutted out of the creek. Nothing was left but the bare rigs of the rocks and the big trees. In a single month the whole population drifted away. I had never known there was such a house as this up the creek. But, for that matter, there was a whole lot about the creek and the creek people that nobody ever knew for certain. For a couple of years a thousand things happened every day along that little run of water. There were enough murders and excitement of all kinds to fill a book every week. One thing piled on top of the other, and the heads of people were too filled to retain everything.

However, there was the house as big as life; and the clattering of the hammers came from inside of it. Out in front there was a litter of lumber and some homemade sawbucks, with a drift of yellow sawdust lying on the ground and sparkling almost like the glittering gold itself.

I didn't need more than that to explain everything. The last eight-mule load of lumber had gone to this same spot; and the carpenters were using up the last of it to fit up the inside of the house, while Buck Logan brought on more stuff to polish off the job. That was enough explanation for any man; I mean, that was enough surface explanation, though underneath the surface there was as much of a mystery as ever. Why people would want to come out here to the end of the world, beat me.

I soon learned that the two carpenters who had been so busily at work were Roger Beckett and Zack Morgan. And I learned, also, that it was to be my job to guard the house against intruders.

But how was I to go about guarding the place, since that was my duty?

I talked it over with big Buck Logan. My idea was that I should stand guard with guns at hand all day and only knock off for a short sleep at night. It would be hard work, but at the same time it would be some return for the high pay which I was getting. Buck listened to all I had to say, and then he simply smiled at me. He said that it showed my heart was right, but it showed that I was not thinking very straight.

How could I stand guard and shelter the whole house, and men working here and there all around the place, inside and outside? I could stand guard for a year and have a thousand men shot down around me from the shelter of the trees that overlooked the house on all sides.

Yes, that was very true; and I could see it, so I asked Buck to make his own suggestion. He had some, of course. There was never a man to beat Buck for suggestions; he had more ideas than an east wind has drops of rain.

He said that the main thing was for me to take it easy and have a good time.

'How can I sit around and take it easy,' said I, 'when I got the responsibility of the lives of three gents on my hands, and half a dozen murderers waiting out yonder – as you tell me there are – all ready to jump in and cut our throats.'

Buck, he only smiled at me. He said, 'Now, kid, don't go off half cocked, like this. Lemme tell you something that is true and darned true at that. Nobody can really work well until he can work happily, and the picture of you standing up and holding onto a gun all day long ain't a happy picture. I tell you what you do. You like hunting. Now what you should do is to make this a little hunting party. You can't have your eyes open all day and every day, and all night and every night. What I say is that you should just go out and look for game two or three times a day. And when you out regular for game, what always happens? The game is scared away. Well, kid, you can bet your boots that this two-legged game that we're talking about will be scared away, too – or at least, it will get dog-goned cautious. It will see signs of your tramping around this here place in a big circle. And it will make them pretty cautious.

'Now, what I'd suggest is that you go out about three times – and that you pick the times when folks generally start out on deviltry. They go out in the morning, in the half light, to commit a lot of their crimes. And then they go out in the evening again. And besides that, of course, the time that they like best of all is the night. So I suspect that you'd better make a round in the mornings. Just loop around through the trees and zigzag so that you cover a couple of miles, keeping your eyes open all of the time. After that you take your time off and loaf along until the evening. And when the evening comes, you can make another trip, and the same some time during the night.'

'Look here, Buck, you want me to go hunting at night?'

'I'm not asking you to hunt painters or coons,' said Buck. 'All I'm asking you to do is to ward off men from us; and if it's hard for you to see at night, it will be hard for them, too. I've an idea that you might have a lot more luck by night than you have by day.'

This gave me something to think about; but after all it wasn't very hard to see that Buck, as usual, was pretty right. If I stood around with a gun all day long, what would I be except a mark for them to shoot at? But if I traipsed around through the forest in the evening and in the morning – that is to say, in the hunting times when all the beasts turn out in the woods – then it would be a good deal different. I might have luck.

I said, 'Here's another little thing. Suppose I do come across somebody. What do I do?'

'Shoot!' said Buck. 'Do I have to tell you that?'

'Shoot without no warning given?' says I.

'Why the devil should you give a warning?'

'Buck,' says I, 'I see that you got an idea that I'm just a butcher – which I ain't at all. Gents have got to be warned away from this valley before they're shot down, and how is this to be arranged?'

'You're getting so particular, kid,' said Buck, 'that I dunno how you're goin' to be useful. What chance is there of anybody but crooks being stirring around here?'

'Not much chance,' said I.

'Not one chance in a million,' says Buck. 'No, sir, and you know that. Who ever comes here to the Daggett Valley? Since the last of the gold was washed out, nobody comes here. You couldn't find a man here with a fine-toothed comb, except for the throat cutters that would like to get rid of the whole mob of us; so you're just talking through your hat uncommon loud and long, old son.'

Well, there was a good deal in what he said. I thought it all over and I asked him how far the property ran that his boss – the folks that owned the old house on the hill – had a claim to in the valley. Buck pointed out the boundaries to me. It was a right smart piece of land, too, I can tell you.

I mapped out a regular beat for myself; and the first time I made the round, I spent a lot of time setting out the signs on which I had made up my mind. Those signs were flat, thin pieces of big board that I nailed onto trees where they could be seen easy, and on every board there was a few words in black paint:

PRIVATE PROPERTY
NO TRESPASSING

That was a sign that I could remember seeing and hating when I was a boy, because it had always looked sort of poisonous and mean, you know. But I figured that, with those signs up, there would be a lot more excuse for me if I was to turn loose and pepper any strangers with powder and lead.

Buck, he let me do all of these things; and he agreed with me that it was the best way, and that it was making our game more aboveboard.

When I had finished putting up those signs and making my round, it was a good first day's work; and I was satisfied. I had stuck up about a dozen of those boards at all of the most prominent places, so that it would be pretty near impossible for folks that followed any of the natural trails toward the old house to fail to see those signs and read the warning that was on them. It was my duty, as near as I could make out. When I had done that I had another talk with Buck and Zack and Roger Beckett; and they all three agreed with me that from that time on, if I found any folks inside of the limits of those signs, I wouldn't have to stop and ask any questions. I could just haul off, and turn loose on them, and drop them if I could.

Besides, you see that the ground that I had fenced off with my warnings wasn't all of the property that belonged to the owner of the house, according to Buck Logan. It really wasn't more than a quarter or a fifth of the whole layout. But even so, it was big enough to make a stiff walk three times each twenty-four hours.

When I started making these rounds, things settled down at once, the two gents who were working at the repairing of the house, their nerves got more quieter; and you would think that I hadn't just started walking my rounds – you would think that I had fenced in that place with a wall of brass half a mile high.

VI

The Bullet From Ambush

I was getting ready for my morning round, several days later, when Buck Logan came down to me with a yellow face covered with wrinkles and shadows around his eyes, like a man who hasn't slept for weeks.

He said, 'This is the big day, Doc.'

'All right,' said I. 'If this is the big day, tell me what my part in it is to be.'

'Get your Jupe hoss,' said Buck, 'and start drifting over toward the edge of the valley – the same road that we come in by. Go to that road and wait there till you see a covered wagon coming – an old-fashioned schooner. When you see that, ride up to it; and you'll find a little gent with a pointed gray beard sitting up driving, and along with him there'll be an old gent with long white hair and a tolerable pretty girl. You ride right up to them, and likely you'll have a gun held onto you, but don't be scared by that. It'll simply mean that the gent with the gray beard is playing safe. You go on up with your hands over your head and say that I sent you to him.'

'What name shall I call him?' I asked.

'Names ain't any matter,' said Buck Logan. 'You don't need no names. Just give my name when you come up, and that'll be enough. But after that, mind that you don't do too much talking.'

'All right,' said I, 'I can get along without talking. But what am I to do about the wagon and the folks that are in it?'

He said, 'Your job is to get that wagon safe down through the trees and up the valley to the house, here. You understand?'

'I understand,' said I.

'And one of the main things is for you to get it here not before sunset. You hear?'

He counted out these things with a frown, stabbing at the palm of his hand with his forefinger.

I nodded. I couldn't make out why the wagon had to get to the old house after sunset time, but then that went along with a flock of other things that I didn't understand. I was getting used to being in a sort of a mist. I had, in all my time there, only learned that the chief one from whom we expected a lot of trouble, was named Grenville.

'Does Grenville want to stop that wagon?' I asked Buck.

He shook his head. 'I dunno,' said he. 'Maybe

Grenville does, and maybe he don't. Just what goes on inside of his head I can't make out; but, if he does suspect what those folks mean to us, he'll make the biggest try in the world to stop the rig. You understand?'

I nodded.

'I mean, he'll try killing,' said Buck Logan.

'All right,' said I. 'The three of you stay here. I go out to bring in a wagon where there's a girl, a white-haired old man, and only one gent able to use guns – and him no youngster, as far as I can make out. I may have the whole gang of Grenville on my back!'

Buck nodded again. 'Of course you may,' said he; 'there's no doubt about that. You're playing a dangerous game, to-day. But I'll tell you what, I'd almost as soon have your job at the wagon as have you away from the house this morning. If Grenville don't hit at you and the folks on the wagon, he's pretty apt to hit at me and the boys that are here with me.'

He seemed pretty serious about it, and Buck was not of a nature to take trouble any more serious than it had to be taken.

'All right, Buck,' said I, 'this is the beginning of the big play, then?'

'The beginning of the big play,' he said, still as solemn as an owl.

'So long!' says I.

'So long!' says Buck, and turned on his heel.

So I went and got my Jupe hoss and rode down

the valley.

I was so glad that the misery was gonna be over, danger or no danger, that I could have sung; and I did sing, as I went ramping along, as though there was not the least mite of danger in the world from Grenville and his clan.

This was the way I was feeling then – pretty proud and pretty gay – as I worked my way down through the woods, keeping to the old wagon trail and not making any particular effort to keep Grenville or any of his lookouts from spotting me.

When I look back to it, I wonder how any man could of been so plumb foolish as I was, when I started out. As if I hadn't been warned enough. No, you would think I had never been in that valley before, and that I didn't know there was such a person as Grenville in the whole wide world.

Well, we came to the place on the trail where there had been a bridge; but the bridge that crossed the old gully had busted down, long ago, and the wreckage of the wagon that had busted it down lay there in the hollow. The heavy ironwork of the wagon, that hadn't been washed away in the spring freshets, had lodged among the rocks. The trail itself had swung aside, instead of rebuilding the wrecked bridge. The trouble had happened, I suppose, along toward the end of the mining days when it was hardly worth while repairing the road.

Anyway, the road dipped to the side and across the gulch at a slant; and just as we got to the middle of the crossing, while I was watching the ground ahead of me, Jupe stopped and whirled to the side. I thought the old fool was refusing on account of a little patch of water, an inch or so deep, that lay in front of us. So I cursed him and give him the spur – but, instead of straightening out, he just threw up his head with a snort; and, as he threw it up, a gun banged from the thicket, and the bullet that was meant for my brain bashed through Jupe's.

VII

Stalking the Stalker

At least, poor Jupe died without pain. He fell so sudden and complete that I didn't have time to free my feet from the stirrups.

Also, I think that the quickness of that fall saved my life a second time. That fellow in the bushes was shooting as straight as he was shooting fast. One bullet combed past my head as Jupe fell, and another spattered dirt in my face as I rolled out of the saddle along the ground. That roll carried me within twisting distance of the brush, and I pitched myself into it just as a fourth bullet came whining for me.

I knew, as I crawled through those bushes, that only fate and Jupe had saved me. And kneeling there in the brush, handling my guns, I knew, too, that in five minutes either I would be dead for sure, or the gent that had tried to murder me would be eating dirt.

I started straight for him. Yes, I was so mad that I went smashing and crashing through the brush, aiming right for the spot from which he had done the shooting – as though he must have used up his bullets, or as though I couldn't be killed with powder and lead!

Anyway, my wits came back to me before I had gone very far. I stopped on the edge of a little depression that couldn't be very far away from the spot where the other gent had laid for me. There was a part of a rotten stump lying on the group in front of me, and I kicked that stump so that it rolled along down the slope and come to rest in the brush straight ahead of me. There it lay, and it had made a sound a good deal like that which a man makes in charging wild, through the woods.

So I thought if the other gent really was near, the noise of that rolling stick might make him think I had ducked down into the brush at the bottom of that dip of ground.

Leastwise, if he was thinking that, there was nothing to keep me from taking him from behind.

I went slithering along as soft as I was able to work, and thanking Heaven for the breeze which come rustling and talking through the tops of the trees. That wind made about enough sound to drown out all the noise I was making. So I worked myself in a circle that brought me through a thick standing hedge of young poplars.

And then my heart jumped into my throat; for there he was, stretched out along the ground and turned away from me, with his rifle at the ready, trained on something before him and beneath him. I knew he was searching the hollow into which I had rolled the bit of stump.

I raised up easy and stepped through the trees. I didn't want to take no advantage of him; and so I figured that if I put my Colt into the holster and called out a warning to him, it would make about an even thing of it – his rifle against the surprise that I was giving him.

I did just that. I sneaked my revolver back into the holster; but just as I did that, something seemed to pop into his head and make him uneasy, because all at once he lifted up his head and stiffened all through his body.

'You houn' dog!' I snarled at him through my teeth.

I was thinking of the way that poor old Jupe had died for me – and just then it looked to me as though no man's life was more than enough to be paid down for that little old cutting hoss of mine.

When he heard my voice, he pitched himself right around and snatched his gun to his shoulder. I was half of a mind that, when he heard a voice like that behind him, he would stick up his hands, but there wasn't any quit in that man. He started for me like I was nothing at all, and almost before I could wink, the long barrel of that rifle was flashing at my eyes.

I yanked out my Colt. I didn't have time to take any aim or draw any bead. It was just a case of a snapshot from the hip, in case I wanted to get in something before he planted me with an aimed bullet; so I fired from the hip the instant I had flopped my Colt out.

The shot hit the gravel just in front of him and brought out a yell and a gasp. His rifle went off, but the bullet rattled through the branches, a long distance away from me. He jumped to his feet and threw his hands across his face.

He was blinded a bit. And, instead of shooting him down, I thought that it might be a pretty good thing if I closed in on him and took him a prisoner – because then he could act as a sort of hostage for us and maybe keep Grenville from trying to murder us from behind the brush.

So I ran in at him, full of this new idea.

It would have been easy, if he had really been blinded, but he wasn't. He saw me coming and wrenched at his Colt. He got it out of the holster, but just then I reached for him with my fist and managed to hit his jaw. He went down on his back with a thump and a grunt, and the Colt clanged on the rocks.

No, he wasn't done fighting yet. As he lay there he kicked out and knocked my feet out from under me. Down I fell right on top of him, and, believe me, it was like falling on the top of a wild cat. He was just a mite faster than chain lightning and a little bit stronger than a tiger. But as I fell, I got a throat hold. He whanged at my face, and he tore at my hands; he was so strong that in half an instant he was on top of me, and I was under him. But before he could use that advantage, my grip told on him. His face blackened, his eyes turned up in his head, and he went limp and soft.

I rolled him off and threw a handful of water in his face from my canteen. And I saw him come to by steps and stages, and you might say, just pulling himself together by degrees, so I sat up and shook myself to see where I was hurt.

I can tell you that had been an exciting little whirl, while it lasted; but, when I had gathered myself together, there was the other chap sitting up and beginning to blink at me. I blinked at him, too; and I was terrible surprised by what I seen, because here was the red hair and the fine, handsome features which I had been told 'Red' Grenville had.

'Look here,' said I, 'are you any relation of Henry Grenville?'

'Perhaps I am,' says he, and he began to brush the leaves and the dirt out of his hair, as cool as you please.

'Well,' said I, 'I was half of a mind that I would take you along with me alive. Now that I see that you come of decent blood, and that you should know better than to shoot from cover – why, curse you, I got a mind to plant a slug between your eyes and leave you here.'

He smiled straight into my face. There was a ton of nerve in him.

'How long,' says he, 'have gun fighters like you been in the habit of talking about fair play and not shooting from cover?'

It was a facer for me. I listened, and I wanted to shoot him full of holes, I can tell you; but I managed to control myself – I don't know how. I said to him:

'I'll tell you, old-timer, that wherever you've learned your stuff about me, you've learned it wrong.'

'Bah!' says he. 'How many men have you shot down from behind a wall? And how many have you shot through the back?'

I let out a yell, it made me so mad. 'You young fool!' I shouted at him. 'If I shot men from behind, why didn't I shoot you down that way – when I had the chance to take you helpless from behind, just now – instead of giving you a little more than a fair break for your life?'

'Why–' said he, and then he stuck.

In the excitement of things happening so fast and so close together, I suppose he had not had a chance to think things over exactly as they happened; but now he frowned and looked as though this think he had just thought about made him a little unhappy.

'I don't care about that,' he said, rather sullenly. 'The fact is that Henry has told us that you're worthy to be hunted like a dog – and that's my excuse – and that's excuse enough.'

'Henry Grenville told you that?'

'Yes,' says he. 'I suppose that you'll call him a liar?'

I didn't answer. I seen that there was no use in arguing with him over a thing like this. The main thing was that I had a brother of Henry Grenville that I could use as a sort of hostage. And I could just about swear that Henry would stop the shooting from behind trees, from this point on.

'Stand up!' says I. 'Stand up and get ready to march.'

'I'm ready here,' said he. 'I'd as soon pass out here as anywhere, but I don't think that I'll march for you.'

VIII

Forward March

It took me a moment or so to understand that this young fool had it fixed in his mind that I was going to murder him before I got through.

When I had digested that idea for a minute, I looked him in the eye; and I said, 'Grenville, what's your first name?'

'Lawrence,' says he, as cool as ever.

'Lawrence,' says I, 'lemme tell you that your brother may be a blooming angel so far as truth telling may be concerned, and I may be the worst black rat in the world; but the fact is, old-timer, that I ain't going to murder you. Not to-day, that is– Maybe to-night I'll cut your throat, and may be to-morrow I'll shoot you through the back; but to-day, I've took a fancy to letting you live, y'understand? And if you care to eat a couple of more squares, you'll buck up and do what I tell you. But, if the next few hours ain't got nothing in store for you, why, I'll polish you off right here and now.'

He listened to me as though I was speaking a foreign language that he didn't understand. But finally he said, 'Well, I'll let you have it your own way. Where do you want me to march to?'

'Where I tell you,' said I; and I guided him back through the woods to the spot where my poor Jupe hoss lay.

Says I, 'This is what you done, Larry, my boy.'

'He threw his head up,' says this cool cucumber. 'Otherwise you'd be lying there, and he'd be eating grass – with an empty saddle.'

I couldn't help admiring this young fool of a boy, in a way. Nobody but a courageous idiot, that didn't care whether or not he lived, would talk like this to a man who had the drop on him. But it was plain to be seen that courage ran pretty thick in the blood of the Grenvilles.

I said, 'Yes, you meant that bullet for me; but maybe while you was shooting at me you murdered something that was a lot better than me – if you admit that a hoss can be better than a man.'

'Ah,' says he, with a quick look aside at me, 'don't I admit that, though? I do! And I've known the horses – and the men.' And he laughed with a sudden sort of enthusiasm.

I began to take more and more of a liking for him. Even if he had been taught to shoot from behind trees – well, there was something decent about him in spite of that.

'Look here, Grenville,' said I, 'this here Jupe hoss was the best cutting hoss I ever rode on. And he was the gamest hoss on the trail that you ever seen.'

'He's a pretty little rabbit,' said Grenville.

'Rabbit?' says I. 'That rabbit, you bonehead, would carry two hundred pounds at a canter nearly all day long. He's stood between me and a rotten sort of a death more times than once. Do you think that the fact that he died for me makes me feel any easier about it, or any kinder to you, Grenville?'

All the time that I said this he wasn't looking at the horse, he was looking at me; and when I finished, he said, 'Willis, if I'd been you – well – Larry Grenville would be a dead man.'

'Well,' said I, 'there was never a time from the beginning of the world when shooting from behind brush done any real good. It's got me a dead hoss, and I think that you're decent enough to have it give you a few bad nights during the rest of your life. Now help me get the saddle off of him.'

He started to work without a word. We stripped everything off of Jupe, and then he pointed to a tower of loose rock that heaved up on the bank just above the spot where Jupe lay in the hollow. I took that for a pretty good hint; and we heaved away side by side until that tower toppled, and three or four tons of rock went crashing and sliding over the spot where Jupe was and buried him from sight complete.

After that it was easier to go along on my trail, but Larry was a pretty silent boy for the rest of the way. He didn't have nothing to suggest, and his head hung pretty low.

Suddenly he broke out, as we turned onto the up slope that pointed toward the edge of the valley, 'Henry was all wrong about you, Willis.'

'I'll tell you why,' said I. 'I would be a lot more use to him dead than living. You can write that down for facts. Step out, kid; I'm overdue.'

We swung down that trail for another couple of miles, until we come to the edge of the green; and there was the whiteness and the oven heat of the desert before us.

'What d'you aim to do with me?' asked Larry Grenville.

'I aim to keep you with me,' I said, 'as a sort of a promise that while you're here, Henry won't try his hand at any more Indian fighting. Is that fair?'

He nodded right away. 'That's fair,' he said.

'And if you try to break away – why, I'll treat you the way you treated my little old Jupe hoss. Is that square?'

'The squarest thing in the world,' said he. 'And darn it, Willis, I feel as though this was a black day in my life.' And he went on with a frown on his face, thinking hard all of the time.

We kept on for about another hour, and then I made a halt on the edge of one of the low sand hills where we could get at something that served as an excuse for shade – I mean, we sat down in the skeleton shadow of a group of Spanish daggers. And we let the perspiration come trickling down our faces while I started off to the horizon across the flashing and shining heat waves of the desert.

By what big Buck Logan had said, I had guessed that I would find the covered wagon coming over the hills early in the morning; but it was pretty near to noon before I saw a little spot of white against the sky, like a cloud brushing across the face of the earth.

'What's that?' asked Larry.

'More trouble for your brother is what it looks like to me,' I told him.

He stared and stared, but he wouldn't ask any more questions.

Then I said, 'Look here, Larry, do you know the thing that brought your brother up here to Daggett Valley?'

'Of course,' says he, with a quick look to the side at me.

'Is it worth the trouble that he's taking?' I asked.

'That all depends,' said Lawrence Grenville. 'The money might be worth the trouble to him, but the fun would be worth the trouble to me.'

'And do the gents that are working for Henry figger on getting in on a split of the loot?'

'They work by the day,' said Larry; 'but why do you ask me this stuff?'

'I wanted to see,' said I, 'how big a business man he was.'

In the meantime the dust cloud was floating across the hills toward us; and now that cloud lifted a little, and I could see through the film of it the outlines of the arched back of the wagon, and then four animals that was pulling the load. It couldn't be a very heavy load, because they came along at a fast walk; and they did not stop at the inclines, as Buck Logan had stopped his mule team when he worked our way across the same trail.

Now the thing came closer and closer. It was one of those old-fashioned wagons such as they used to use, in the gold days, for making voyages around on the prairie and across the barren desert.

Grenville stood up and peered at them. 'It looks odd,' said he. 'What are they doing with one of those clumsy old things?'

'Why,' said I, 'maybe they're on the track of the same trouble that brought your brother into Daggett Valley. Come on down with me and we'll hail them.'

He stepped out from the shadow along with me, but as we got down into the trail there was a shout from in front of us. I saw the mules stop, and I saw a rifle leveled at us in the hands of a man with a gray, pointed beard.

Buck was a true mind reader, right enough!

Meeting the Prairie Schooner

'You've walked us into a bunch of lead,' said Larry Grenville. 'I thought you were a friend of this gang?'

It was a fact. The gray-bearded fellow looked pretty wicked behind that rifle of his, but we hoisted up our hands and walked in to talk to the tiger face to face. When we got to the heads of the leading span of mules he stopped us again.

'Now who are you?' he asked me.

'I am Doc Willis,' said I.

He snapped. 'Where's your horse?'

'Dead,' said I.

'Dead where?'

'Dead in Daggett Valley,' said I.

'And you walked on here?'

'Yes.'

'With good news or bad?'

'With no news worth talking about,' said I.

'Keep your hands up,' said he; 'and let your partner back up a bit.'

I told Grenville to do as he was ordered; and he backed out of the way, while the gray-beard climbed down from his seat and came up to me. As soon as he was on the ground he didn't look half so impressive as sitting down. He was one of those short-legged, long-waisted fellows. I suppose he didn't stand taller than me; but seated, he looked like a six-footer, at least. He came toward me with a sort of a wabble in his stride, because he was very bow-legged.

'Now,' said he, speaking quietly when he came up to me, 'tell me where you stand; and you don't have to shout it.'

I said, 'Buck Logan sent me out here to meet you.'

'To meet who?' said he.

'A girl, a white-haired old gent, and a gray-bearded fellow in a covered wagon.'

'And what names did Buck tell you they wore?'

'Buck told me no names.'

He frowned again at this. 'What did Buck mean by that?' he growled.

'You can answer that better than me,' said I.

'What's your job with Buck?' he asked me.

'Me?' said I. 'I'm the chore boy and I carry water for the real men.'

'Don't talk smart,' says the gray-bearded gent. 'That will win you nothing with me. I asked you what you were doing for Buck.'

'Fifty dollars' worth a week,' said I.

He canted his head a little to one side.

'Buck is paying big wages, then,' said he.

'That's all in the way you look at it,' I told him. 'It looked good to me at first, but now it looks fairly small.'

'Humph!' says he.

'Humph!' says I.

'Bear a civil tongue in your head,' says he. 'Do you know who I am?'

'I don't give a darn who you are,' says I. 'A gray beard ain't a title, not in this part of the world.'

I thought that that would get a flare out of him, but instead he let a smile come halfway on his lips.

'You don't get fifty a week for that sort of talk,' said he.

'No,' said I, 'I get fifty a week for riding herd on the rest of them and keeping the chills away.'

'Humph!' says he. 'Then you're the killer that Logan was to try to hook up with?'

'Am I the killer?' says I, getting madder and madder. 'Well, in my part of the country folks ain't so fond of calling me that.'

'Oh,' says he. 'I'll be polite to you, if that's what you want. And what was your name again?'

'Willis,' says I; and, as I look him over, I feel that there ain't anybody that I ever met that I liked less than this fellow. He was about as cold as ice; and his eyes had a way of going snicker-snack, right through you and finding out what was on your insides.

'Willis,' says he, 'you came out to guard us into

the valley, I suppose; but you don't know who I am?'

'I don't,' said I. 'And I don't—'

'Leave that out,' he broke in, as cool as ever, but smiling a little again, 'but you might as well know me now. I'm Alston.'

'Alston?' says I. 'Then I suppose that the old white-headed gent on the seat, yonder, is Carberry?' For I'd heard some mention of a gent by the name of Carberry being mixed up in this affair.

He gave a start and a blink. 'Carberry? Why, don't you know–' began Alston.

Then he stopped himself and stared at me, like a man would at a fellow who said that the earth was flat.

'No,' said I, 'I never had the pleasure of meeting up with Carberry. Who is he? President?'

'Maybe you'll be ready to vote for him in that job,' says the gray-beard, 'before you get through with this game. Now, who is the fellow who's with you?'

'Don't you like him?' says I.

'Don't be sassy, Willis,' says Alston; 'tell me who he is. I have a right to know, because I won't take another step into the valley without knowing who I have along with me.'

'All right,' I replied to him, 'I don't mind telling you that he is the gent that dropped my Jupe hoss.'

He took another quick look at young Larry Grenville, and then he took a long look at me and seemed to be really seeing me for the first time.

'The man who killed your horse – how?'

'From behind a tree.'

'And you got him?'

'There he is!'

'But you didn't scalp him, eh?'

'Alston,' said I, getting madder and madder, 'whether you like the looks of me, or I like the looks of you ain't a matter of any importance; but what really counts is that I ain't a killer, and that I won't be talked to like one. And I want you to write that down in red letters and never to forget it. I don't kill gents for the sake of keeping my hand in.'

'Very hot!' says Alston, nodding at me, and looking me over like I was a horse or a dog. 'All right. I won't rub your hair the wrong way. Only – what do you intend to do with the man? What's his name?'

'Grenville,' said I.

I thought that might get a little more attention from him, but I didn't expect it to make him stagger. He reached out and gripped my arm, and there was a lot more power in that hand of his than I had thought. By the feel of that grip of his, I peeled ten years off my guess of his age. No, he wasn't as old as the gray beard had made him look – not by a long ways.

'Henry Grenville!' says he. 'That's not possible! And yet – I can half remember the face; and there is the red hair. Good heavens, Willis, if that's Grenville, our troubles are all ended.'

'Are they?' I snarled at him, because I hated him every minute more and more. 'Well, he's Grenville, all right, but his first name isn't Henry.'

'Not Henry? The devil!'

I told him that the name of this fellow was Lawrence, but here Alston pricked up his ears again. He said that next to having Henry himself, this capture was best, because with it, we could tie the hands of Henry himself pretty effectually. He said that we would put Larry into the wagon, and that he, Alston, would keep guard over him, while the old chap drove the wagon along the road and I went on ahead to scout for trouble.

'Because,' said Alston, 'when Henry finds out that his brother has disappeared, he'll come shouting for trouble; and when he starts to make trouble, he's very apt to finish the job that he begins.'

Then he took me back toward the wagon.

'Don't mind the old boy,' says he. 'He's pretty safe and sane, to-day. But I had a rocky time with him on Wednesday.'

While he led me up toward the seat, we took another look for Larry. I hadn't been watching him very close, because it would be hard for him to get away. He had no gun with him, now; and, if he tried to break away, it would be dead easy for me to pick him off before he had got very far through that loose surface of sand.

Well, there hadn't been any idea in the mind of Larry of escaping. And now there he was, leaning beside the driver's seat, as calm as you please, smoking away at a cigarette and making conversation with the old fellow and the girl.

They made a picture, I can tell you, Larry Grenville, almost handsomer than any man had a right to be, standing there with his head thrown back, and the girl leaning above him and laughing down to him – and she prettier than any I had ever seen. The old chap, he sat back with his hands folded in his lap, smiling at Larry, and smiling at the girl, but with his eyes mostly fixed far off on the horizon, and his smile not meaning a great deal of anything. I could see that he was only about half or a quarter with us. Sickness and death had begun at the top, with him. And when I come up close and looked up into his thin, kind, old face, with the white hair streaming down around it, a wave of pity come over me which I've never recovered from to this day. I would have cut off an arm to make the old chap smile with a bit of life in his face.

Alston did the introducing in a pretty free and easy way.

'Lou Wilson,' says he to the girl, 'this is Willis. And,' says Alston, 'Doc, this is William Daggett.'

I had thought there couldn't be many more surprises crowded into this day of my life. From the beginning right straight, there had been something happening every little while; but this was the crown of everything. For here was a name that had passed from reality and become part of a story, all through that section of the West. Here was the man that had struck gold on the creek. Here was the man that had struck the gold and started the rush that crowded Daggett Creek, in a little while, with miners gouging through the earth to get rich. Here was the man, too, who had built the house on the hill that Buck had been working so hard to get into shape and freshen up and make like new.

And what was he? Why, the man that had done all of these things and made so much history, he was just a hollow husk. Once there had been a man inside of him, but now he was like a light that has burned low and is about to flicker out. And there was a flicker in the blue eyes of Daggett, as he smiled down at me – a quiet, sad, feeble sort of a light that made me almost sorry that I was alive.

'I'm proud to know you, Mr Daggett,' said I. 'I've just been up in the valley where you—'

Here Alston stepped heavily on my foot.

But I hadn't made any break, so far as the old fellow was concerned. He just smiled and nodded at me and said, 'Exactly! Exactly! And what a world it is, Mr Wallis! What a world it is, Mr Wallis!'

Even my name, which he'd heard half a minute before, he couldn't remember; and now his old blue eyes wandered off to find their favorite spot on the horizon.

Lou Talks

Alston wanted for me to handle the team while he watched Grenville in the wagon, and I said that I would; but not being used to handling four reins, I jumped up onto the rear leader and started to guide the team that way, reining the leaders the way I wanted them to go. But before we had rolled a hundred yards, somebody yipped on the far side of the off leader; and there was Lou, sitting sidewise on the off leader, and laughing at me, as easy and as companionable as you please.

I looked back to the wagon, and it amused me a good deal to see it bothered two of them a lot to watch the girl out there riding the mule at my side. It bothered young Larry Grenville, for one. And it bothered the gray-beard, too.

Lou hooked a thumb back over her shoulder.

'How did you ever happen to pick up with this gang of thugs?' said she.

'I was gonna ask you the same thing,' said I.

'You was?' says Lou. 'Well, I asked you first. Let's have what you got to say for yourself.'

'Suppose,' said I, 'that you was a cow-puncher.'

'Yes,' says she.

'And suppose that you was out of a job, and wondering what gang you would pick on with next, and suppose the most you ever got for riding range was about forty bucks a month–'

'I know,' said she.

'And then a gent drives by with an eight-mule load of lumber and he says. "Come along with me and get your fifty bucks a week, and all you got to do is to ride herd on a couple of gents that I've got at work" – why what would you have said, Lou?'

'I would of said, "Come take me quick, before you get a chance to change your mind." What did you say, Doc?'

'I told him that I didn't want his game, and I let him roll on out of my sight; but after he was gone, I just couldn't stand it. Along in the middle of the day I went pelting along after him, and so – here I am, still riding around in circles, and still in the dark.'

'In the dark,' she says, with her husky voice suddenly barking at me. 'Did I hear you straight?'

'You heard me straight,' I told her.

She straightened around so that she could look fairly and squarely at me. It was a strange thing, but when you faced Lou you could see the thoughts working in her eyes. Not just what they were, of course; but you could see her eyes brighten and darken, and you could see the color change from blue to gray and back again. I never seen such a pair of eyes in my life, and neither did any other man.

'Say, Doc,' said she, 'maybe you're an innocent, poor, young boy that's being dragged into this dirty deal sort of against his will.'

'Maybe I am not,' says I, laughing back at her when I saw her drift. 'I ain't asking you for any of your pity, Lou.'

'Thanks,' says she. 'That's one strain off my mind. But what do you mean by saying that you're riding around in the dark?'

'Ain't that plain English?' said I.

'Don't get huffy,' says she. 'I'm not riding you.'

'You give a pretty good imitation of it. What are you driving at?'

'You ain't a baby. How could they ring you in with your eyes closed?'

'I'm a hired man, here, not a boss.'

That seemed to surprise her.

'If they get in gents like you for the hired-man parts,' said she, 'this is quite a show – bigger, even, than I thought.'

'And how big did you think?' I asked her.

'Oh, I don't know. Hundreds of thousands, I suppose.'

'What makes you suppose that?'

'Are you pumping me?'

'Not a bit more than you want to talk, Lou.'

She nodded. It was easy to see that she had her eyes open all the time, but she didn't want to be hostile.

'I don't see any reason why you and me shouldn't be friends, Doc.'

'None in the world,' said I. 'I'm keeping a tight hold on myself to keep from being too friendly too quick.'

She frowned at me. 'What might you mean by that?'

'I'll explain later, when I know you better,' I told her.

'Well,' said Lou, 'have you told me all you know?'

'Oh, no,' said I; 'I don't mind letting you know what I've gathered. It ain't much.'

'Fire away,' said she.

'Well, all I know is that Buck Logan brought me up here.'

'I've heard about him,' said she. 'What sort is he?'

'Square,' said I. 'A big gent, slow-speaking, usually – and honest, I think.'

'But you ain't sure?'

'I'm sure of nothing in this game.'

'Not even of me?'

I looked into those wonderful, queer, changing eyes of hers. 'Not even of you.'

I thought that this might anger her a little, but there was nothing soft about that girl.

'All right,' said she, 'that doesn't make me mad. It's gonna be pretty easy to talk to you, Doc. So you don't even know Buck Logan?'

'I don't. I thought I did. I still feel mighty friendly toward him. But lately I've got the idea that this business means a lot more to him than any friendship would.'

'No friend would stand between him and the cash he expects to get out of the deal?'

'That's right. That's about the way I figure it.'

'Is Logan inside of the deal?'

I thought it over for a minute; then I said, 'It seems to me that Logan must know about as much as anybody. But I'm not sure even of that. He may be only a hired man, as far as I know. I'm sure of nothing.'

'Go on,' says she.

'Well, then, I know that up there in the valley there's Henry Grenville, a gentleman with education, and all that. And he's got a crowd of gun fighters with him, and he's gunning to get something out of the deal.'

'Is that all you know about him?'

'That's about all. Then there's something about the old Daggett house. Do you know what it is?'

'The Daggett house?' said Lou. 'No. What has a house to do with it?'

'A lot. I see that there's a lot you don't know, Lou; but, take it from me, when this thing is opened up and explained, the old Daggett house will have a lot to do with the explanation. At least, that's the way Buck Logan and his crew are expecting it to happen. But they ain't sure. I can see that Buck ain't sure. He's working in the dark, and he don't know just where he's going. And I can see the worry of it in his face all the time.'

She nodded, thinking of everything that I had to say.

'Then, behind this thing, or mixed up in it I don't know how, there's you and old Daggett. You can tell me something about that. Then somewhere in the yarn there is Carberry—'

'What Carberry?'

'The bandit.'

'Carberry, the bandit? Oh, he's dead a long time ago,' said Lou.

'Dead!' I shouted at her. 'Why, Lou, then his ghost is back in this business and using his hand somewhere and in some way. I know that for certain.'

'Go on,' said Lou; 'this is pretty interesting.'

'I've got to the end of my rope,' said I. 'I used to think, at first, that there was something hidden in the bottom of the house; but, if that was the case, I suppose they would tear the old place to pieces and find out what it was. Anyhow, the thing they're looking for must be so big that it couldn't be hidden in a nutshell; even if it was pure solid gold, it would have to take up a good deal of room.'

'Why,' said Lou, 'maybe they're looking for some sort of a paper.'

'Humph!' said I. 'That sounds a good deal too much like a book to convince me.'

'May be it does,' she admitted; 'but we got to try everything, if we want to hope to hit on the right trail, here.'

I admitted that that was right. Then I told her how the old house was being fixed up, and she wondered at that no end. She couldn't make head nor tail out of it, because she agreed with me that nobody would fix up a big house like that just to live in, with Daggett Creek so far from the rest of the world. And what the hidden purpose could be was a sticker.

It was good to talk these things all over with her, because she was as smart as a whip; and she thought three thoughts while I was thinking one.

Then I asked her what she knew about Alston, because he seemed to be as high up in the deal as anybody.

She thought for a minute before she answered, and then she said, 'Well, I'll tell you about Alston. I've known some crooks in my day. I've known cattle rustlers and yeggs. Dad was free and easy, and he never cared who came and tapped at his door and asked for a meal and a place to sleep. I've seen some pretty hard cases around our house; but I'll tell you what – the lowest, the meanest, the sharpest, the smartest, and the wickedest of the lot is that gambler, Alston!'

I sort of knew beforehand just what she would say, somehow. I'd felt all of those things about him.

I couldn't help breaking out, 'It's pretty good to hear you say that, Lou; because it's easy to see that he don't feel the same way about you as you do about him.'

'He wants me to marry him; and he expects that I

will, when I see how rich this deal will make him. You understand? But I'll be dead before I ever marry him. You can lay your money on that bet.'

Well, that was about the best news I'd ever heard.

XI

Trouble Ahead

I took a while to digest what she'd just told me, and I felt so happy that I couldn't help slapping a mule on the hip and singing out at a rabbit that came hopping across the wagon trail.

'Only,' said I at last, 'that don't tell me how you was rung in on this deal.'

'The reason is back in a bank,' said the girl.

'Money?'

'Nothing but. That's why I'm here – and a good fat stake!'

'I hope so!' I told her.

'Twenty-five hundred iron men is what I corralled before I would go along in the party,' said Lou.

And I blinked at her. 'Why, Lou,' said I, 'it seems to me that old Alston would hardly pay that much for less than a murder.'

'It looks that way, don't it?' said Lou. 'And now

I'll hand you a surprise. He's giving me that money and a lot more, if the deal works, and all for the sake of what?'

'I couldn't guess,' said I.

'All for wearing a funny old dress! Can you beat that?'

No I couldn't beat that; and I was perfectly willing to tell her so.

'All right,' said Lou, 'but that's the fact, strange though you may think it.'

I just looked at her.

'Do you believe me?'

'Lou,' said I, 'I don't know you well enough to tell you how many kinds of a liar I think you are.'

She wasn't mad. She just put back her head and laughed. 'Maybe you're partly right, too,' said she; 'but that's my story, and that is what I've got to stick to.'

'Is that part of the bargain with Alston?'

'Alston? No, he'd probably poison you, if he knew that I'd told you even this much.'

'Who is Alston?'

'Alston,' says Lou, 'is a gent that done what ain't possible.'

'How do you mean?'

'In the old days, you know how the gamblers used to come down to the mining camps and cheat the boys out of their gold dust?'

'I've heard about that; and I've seen some of it, of course.'

'Well, there's a good old saying that there was

never a crooked gambler that didn't go on the rocks sooner or later?'

'Yes.'

'Some of them got cleaned out at cards, when they met up with a worse crook than themselves. Some of them got stabbed in the back, and then some of them was shot down in fair fights and—'

'That's right, and I've seen it happen.'

'But sooner or later, they all go; and their money goes, too, because it comes through their hands too easy to stick, you see?'

'All right,' said I. 'That's all a fact. But what has that to do with Alston?'

'Well, I'll tell you. He's the exception to the rule. He's the one old-time gambler that stayed with the game and that beat it. When he was gambling, he took every chance and played it big – big and crooked, I mean to say. He worked cards, and he worked dice. He knew how to fix up a crooked set of horse races and get the money out of the Indians, even. He knew how to salt up a claim very fine and stick a poor sucker with it. He knew all sorts of things; but, most of all, he was good at the dice, they tell me. He made money out of everything; and, finally, he had the nerve to draw back out of the game that he was in and go East and settle down where he could pretend to be respectable. That was the way with this here Alston.'

'And now this game has brung him out of his shell?'

'That's it! He's got plenty of money. He's living easy. He's showed me a flock of pictures of his horses, and his dogs, and his house, and all of that. He's terribly proud of it; and it's a pretty good place, right enough. But this deal was big enough for the hopes of what he could make in it to bring him out West; and so here he is, and he thinks he'll win – though something tells me that he's taking a long, long chance.'

'What makes you think that?'

'Why, for one thing, he told me that he never had this idea at all, until he seen me.'

That staggered me.

'Until he seen you, Lou?' I gasped at her.

'I was in Denver with an uncle of mine. He went to Denver on a trip. And he seen me there, and hunted me up, and got to know my uncle – just so that he could have a chance to talk to me.'

'When was that?'

'Last year.'

'Been working on this deal ever since?'

'He said that he couldn't do a thing unless I would promise to work with him. And finally he came across with enough money to make me do what he wanted. And here I am, but that's not the only reason. There's old William Daggett, too. I know that poor old fellow is going to be leaned upon a lot by Alston, and you can see for yourself that Mr Daggett ain't to be depended upon. He's only about half here; and the other half is away off – nobody can tell where.'

That was right enough.

'And still,' said I, 'Alston looks like a winner, to me.'

'Sure,' said Lou. 'He says himself that he wasn't a gambler. He was just a gold digger, but he used cards and such things instead of a pick and shovel and got a lot more of the yellow stuff. He wouldn't be in this deal unless there was a fine big chance that he would win with it.'

I looked back into the wagon; and there was Alston sitting steady, with his eyes burning at me, and a bit in front of him was Larry Grenville, looking at me about as mean as old Alston was doing.

No, Alston didn't look like a loser – neither did young Grenville; and the two of them worried me a good deal.

'All right,' said I to Lou. 'There is one pretty sure thing. If Alston is in the deal, it's a crooked one.'

'Maybe, and maybe not,' said Lou. 'I'll think about that when the time comes,' and she began to laugh in her husky, careless way. I liked her fine, but she was still a puzzle to me.

I had something to think about besides the stuff of which we had been talking, pretty soon.

While Lou and me exchanged the little mites of information that we had to give, we had been pushing through miles of sand and passed the green border line just as the sun begun to turn red-gold before falling behind the western mountains. We slid down the first slope; and the leader just brought me over the tip of the next hill – the last hill before we dipped down into the long valley slope – and I had a glimpse, far ahead of me, of a horseman pushing his horse behind a clump of trees.

I didn't ask any questions. I had seen a man, a rifle, and a hoss; and I'd been in Daggett Valley long enough to know that that combination was apt to mean pretty ugly business before many hours had rolled by.

I popped off of the mule, and I ran back beside the driver's seat.

I said, 'Chief, there's one man ahead of us in the trees; and, by the way he acts, I figger that he doesn't want to be seen by us. What do we do now?'

'Turn the wagon around,' said Alston, 'and give the mules the whip.'

I stared up at him. He wasn't the sort of a man to give fool advice like that.

He corrected himself right away.

'No,' said he, 'there ain't room to turn it around. We've got to go ahead or stop.'

'Stop,' said I, 'and they'll have a pretty good chance to bag the whole crew of you.'

He nodded. His eyes were sparkling and snapping and his lower jaw was thrusting out.

'We can't turn around,' said he. 'If we stop, they eat us up. Could we break through them?'

'They're just beyond the top of the next hill,' I told him. 'We couldn't get any speed to drive us over the top of that rise. It don't look big, but it's enough to take all the roll out of our wheels. Besides, the ground is soft, over there; and the wheels will cut in too deep. You couldn't keep up a gallop – not with just these four mules!'

He nodded and swore. 'That sounds like the fact,' he admitted. 'Then there's only one thing left. When the wagon gets down into the hollow, there, it may be that we'll be out of their sight; and, if we are, we got to try to slip out of the wagon and cut away through the trees. Is there much of a chance of that?'

I thought it over.

'One poor chance in ten,' I told him.

'One change in ten is the best chance we have, then,' said he. 'Go get the girl back here into the wagon while I tie the arms of this Grenville.'

XII

Afoot

He kicked on the brakes with his foot, so that the wagon dragged down into the valley very slow and easy; and that gave us a few more seconds of time.

I ran back to Lou and told her to get down and skin for the wagon.

'What's up?' she asked me, as cool as you please.

'Gents with guns,' said I, and waved ahead of me.

'Grenville, I suppose,' said Lou, and jumped from the mule and ran back.

When we got there, we found that there was another obstacle that hadn't been planned on. Old William Daggett didn't understand, and there wasn't time to explain.

He said, 'Gentlemen, gentlemen! If you wish to walk, by all means do so. But I am not very well, and I shall remain with the wagon. It is still some distance to my house, where I hope to make you fairly comfortable; but you will pardon me if I don't accompany you on foot.'

'Poor old man!' said Lou at my ear. 'He thinks he's taking us to his house to entertain us. Make Alston be gentle with him.'

Alston said, 'If I cannot persuade you, I'll have to–' And he reached for Mr Daggett's arm.

I pointed my finger at him like a gun. Well, it stopped him, but he was raving. 'Curse you, what is it?' he barked at me.

'Easy with the old boy!' I told him.

'All right!' said Alston in a fury, jumping down to the ground. 'Leave him behind – and leave all our hopes behind with him. I tell you, you fool, that we can do nothing without him.'

'My dear sirs! My dear sirs!' old Daggett was saying, blinking at us. 'What can it all be about?'

'You try, Lou,' says I.

'There's robbers ahead of us, Mr Daggett!' she cries to him.

'Impossible!' says the old boy.

'Oh, we saw them!'

'In my valley?' says Daggett, very severe. 'Well, well, I shall have to see to that. The rest of you have no fear. It is my pleasure to protect you – and fortunately I am armed.'

With that he pulled out a little, old snub-nosed gat that must have been thirty years old, and he smiled down at it and then at us.

'You see you have nothing to fear,' says he.

And there he sat, very tickled to be in at a fight, with the light beginning to glisten in his eyes, and a spot of color growing in his cheeks.

A very fine, noble-looking old fellow. He was the true grit, all right. It sure warmed my heart to watch him as he sat there with that gun shaking and wabbling about in his old hand.

'Of course you're not afraid, Mr Daggett,' says Lou; 'but we're all afraid. And I'm afraid! You'll come along to take care of me, won't you?'

'God bless me!' says old Daggett. 'My dear child! Of course I'll come along and take care of you. Of course! Of course!'

The wagon had about got down to the foot of the slope as the old chap climbed down to the ground, and in an instant we were all of us in the brush.

The mules went on like nothing had happened at all. And the creaking of the wheels and the crushing of the sand and the gravel under the big iron tires made enough noise to cover the sounds that we made as we combed along through the trees.

We had enough encumbrances, though. There was old man Daggett, of course, still with his gun in his hand, telling everybody to hurry on ahead, while he would bring up the rear and take care that no harm overtook the rest of us. And he had to have Alston on one side of him and me on the other, to help him over the rough places and over the creek, because his legs were so stiff and weak and brittle with age and sickness. Then there was young Grenville. Alston was dead set on not letting him get away, and he kept Grenville in his eye all the time and was talking to him, too.

He said, 'Grenville, mind you, that when I shoot, I haven't got blank cartridges in the gun. You hear me talk? And I'll shoot to kill, as sure as you're a foot high.'

For my part I believed him, and I could see that Grenville believed him too. There was nothing pretty about that Alston. He was mean and hard.

But that wasn't the worst. There was two big bundles, and those Alston insisted on taking along with us. I had to take one of them over my shoulder; and he took the other and waddled along with it, keeping one arm free for old Daggett.

You can see that we couldn't make any particular good time, being bothered and loaded down like this. And now, behind us and above us, we heard a yell of surprise and rage.

The wagon had been stopped, and it was known that we weren't in it. Of course that was the meaning, and there was a secondary meaning that interested us a good deal. By the volume of that roar we knew that there must be at least five or six in the party, and now they would scatter and try to find us.

Well, with five of us making tracks through the woods, how could they help but make a quick find and then come boiling up around us? I said that to Alston, and he nodded and gritted his teeth as he looked back over his shoulder.

'That's like that hound Grenville!' he snarled. 'He knew just when the best time would be for hitting. We should have waited for night before we started to come into the valley.'

'We would have been smashed up in no time,' I told him, 'if we tried to cover this road by the night. Besides, we're not beaten yet; but I think we'll have to fight before we're out of it. Is this why Grenville has been holding off? He's had men enough to eat up the party in the house.'

'Of course! Of course!' snapped Alston. 'What good would it have done him to grab the people at the house until this was there, too!' And he jerked his head toward poor old Daggett who was tottering along between us.

Finally we managed to cover a mile and a half, I should say; and there was no sound of any pursuit behind us. I knew that we would hear them a long time before we could see them. They would be sure to come on horses, and no horse in the world could wind his way silently through such a growth of brush and young sapling as grew through those woods.

We climbed up over the white ridge, where the big stones shoved their knees out of the ground. And then we could look straight ahead through the trees and see in the distance the form of the Daggett house, standing on the hill.

It had a great effect on old Daggett. He threw out his arms toward it, and then he staggered out and away from Alston and me.

'Let him go!' says Alston, frowning and watching very close. 'He's got to get this out of his system some time.'

'Ah, that is the place!'

That was all Daggett would say, over and over, 'Ah, that is the place!' Not a happy tone, like a man seeing an old friend, but a wild, desperate sort of a voice.

'He remembers,' says Alston. 'The old goat remembers more than I suspected!'

We took hold of Daggett, one on either side of him. He gave us a wild look when we came up to him and grabbed him, and he made a faint struggle in our arms.

'Gentlemen,' says he, 'you have come for me, I see.'

'We've come for you,' says Alston.

'Ah, well, I did not think it would be so soon,' said Daggett; 'but there is truth in the saying that blood cries up from the ground, and that murder will out. Murder will out, no matter if it be buried seven leagues under the ground!'

He said it with a real agony in his throat, and I felt a wave of wonder and of fear. Because it didn't seem possible that this old fellow could ever have taken the life of another man.

'However,' says Daggett, 'I confess everything. There will be no need of a cross-questioning. And one of these trees will be quite as good as a scaffold for the hanging of my wretched body. But ah, may God forgive me! In my own house! In my own house!'

I looked at Alston. He was grinning with a sort of cold enjoyment, though the rest of us were all pretty sick. And I was almost glad when, right behind us, we heard horses smashing through the brush.

XIII

Danger Again

Well, as I was saying, that noise of the horses told us that trouble was coming and coming pretty fast. It broke up the concern with which we were watching poor old Daggett and listening to that talk of his that seemed to confess that he had been a murderer. With Grenville and his men smashing up behind us, I hardly knew what to think.

Alston said, 'We got to put in among these rocks and try to stand them off.'

He panted and pointed to a circle of rocks among the trees. But I could see in a minute the weakness of any scheme like that. The rock was all very well for gents on our own level. But what if Grenville and his tribe chose to slip up into the trees and fire down at us? They could butcher the lot of us as easy as if they had us herded into a pen.

But just what could be done looked hard to me to find out, when Lou run up beside me and lifted the bundle from my shoulder, where I was carrying it.

She jerked her head back. 'You'll have to shoo them off, Doc,' says she.

'Look here, Lou,' says I, 'are they a lot of flies, maybe, or deer, do you think?'

She just looked at me; and I knew my medicine; and I took it. I dropped back among the trees with old William Daggett making a terrible scene with Alston. He swore that he would die of shame if anybody but him turned back to face the danger. But they swung on through the trees and I saw no more of them while I looked back to see what sort of trouble would come my way.

Well, it came from two quarters. The gang of Grenville had been split into two sections. And those sections were driving up at us, one on either side of our trail.

The sun was down. I looked up between the great red trunks of the trees at the fire in the sky and the pure, deep blue of it up higher. There was a soft light everywhere, getting dimmer and dimmer; but it was enough light for shooting, and straight shooting, at that.

There were two things that might happen. I might turn loose some lead at the first riders I saw and turn them back, and that would give me a chance to slip away. Or else, when I started shooting, they might come right straight in. That would be the finish of me.

I got me a place not behind one of those whopping big trunks, but in a patch of brush in the center of an open space. From that spot I could see all around me pretty well, and there was enough brush to give me a sort of a screen, especially from men that were snap-shooting from the backs of horses.

I cuddled the butt of my rifle into the hollow of my shoulder and waited. And in another minute I heard horses crashing through the woods to the south of me – not far away, but just comfortably out of sight. I didn't like that. It meant that if I tackled the other lot, this southern mob would swing in and take me from the rear and scoop me up as easy as you please.

But straight before me came the other mischief. I heard some one shouting. I couldn't make out what, because the horses were making so much noise. Then three riders came in a bunch through the trees, with another pair behind them.

Of course by that time I was beginning to wish that I could make back tracks, but it was too late. A lot too late, even if I wanted to lie still, because all five of them were driving straight at the spot where I was lying in the shrubbery.

Well, I began to pull the trigger of that repeater faster than I ever pulled a trigger before in my life, I know. I got a line just above their heads; and I fired three shots before they seemed to realize what was happening; and I fired three more while they made for the trees, all yelling:

'They're yonder in the brush! Scatter, boys!'

They got out of sight with a whoop, I can tell

you; and I almost laughed. But I had no time to spend on laughing. My idea was to get their attention; and then, when they thought they had me at bay, to slip out on the far side of the shrubbery and so leave them there holding the bag, as you might say, with nothing at all in it.

But I needed speed if I was to succeed with that scheme. For I could hear the riders to the south of us shouting and coming on the wing to find out what was causing all the trouble. And all around me the trees were ringing with shouts and with the hoof strokes of the horses on rocks or through crackling brush as they tried to surround me.

I traveled like a snake and a little faster than most snakes, I think; until I got to the edge of the brush and saw before me, not more than six steps to the line of the woods, a flock of strong young saplings growing side by side like so many soldiers standing in a row.

But just as I raised up out of the brush, a rider came out of the trees from the south and with his revolver he put a pair of bullets not more than an inch past my nose. The smell of that lead, I might say, was all I wanted in the way of an argument to convince me that I should get back to the brush as fast as possible.

There were two other riders behind the first man, and one of the two was that same Henry Grenville. They all had their guns out and they threw a pound or two of lead to comb the bushes where I was. One of the slugs stung my leg.

But there wasn't time to see what that wound was. Those three crazy men were driving right at me as though they wanted to ride on top of me, and I had to send a couple of bullets whirring that way before I could check them and send them piling back for the shelter of the trees.

Well, I had them at a distance from me, now. But here they were in a circle around me. And by the way they whooped and carried on, you would have thought they had their hands filled with a treasure. However, it was a bad mess. If they wanted to see me in the open, all they had to do was to touch a match to that brush and let the flames do the rest.

I waited to hear what would happen, and yet I got a small sort of satisfaction from the knowledge that the rest of the party was skimming along through the woods and making fast tracks for the house of Daggett on the hill. They might very well be where I was now, if I hadn't chosen to come back here and turn this trick.

And then it jumped into my mind with a stab of pain that the girl had sent me here. It hadn't been my own idea at all. It had been Lou's hunch. And how could I tell what had made her suggest it? Well, when I had taken that thought home in me, like a bullet, it made me postpone looking at the wound in my leg again. Because the hurt in my heart was a lot greater.

Maybe you have guessed how far the pretty face and the queer, careless way, and the strange eyes, and the husky voice of Lou had carried her with me. Well, I was wild about her. I had known her hardly an hour, and I was already lovesick for the first time.

It was the lowest time in my life, when I began to doubt Lou and her motives. I looked down at my leg, finally, and it wasn't much consolation to me to see that the bullet had only sliced along the surface of the flesh, just above the knee.

In the meantime a voice began calling, 'Alston! Hello, Alston!'

It was the voice of Grenville. If he knew that Alston had been in the party, it showed that he was no fool. He had been taking it easy in the valley, waiting for Alston and his party to come. But from now on, Grenville would cut loose and do business. And things wouldn't be so very easy for the folks up there in the big house – not when they tried to get clear of Daggett Valley. No, that would be the time when they would wish they hadn't thrown me and my guns away!

XIV

Hostages

I waited for another minute until Grenville called again, 'It's no use, Alston. We know we've got you. You might as well talk turkey to me now as later.'

Then I sang out, 'Hello, Grenville! Doc Willis, speaking.'

'Hello, Willis!' he answered me. 'I hear you, but you're not the person I want to talk to just now. Tell Alston that he had better talk for himself.'

Another idea came popping into my head. By this time there had been plenty of minutes for Alston, Daggett, Grenville and Lou to get on to the Daggett house. But if I could show Grenville that they were not with me, he and the rest of his men might pile away on the trail, hoping to catch up with the others. And then that would leave me free to break out.

Or, if only a part of them went, there would be less trouble for me to deal with the ones that were left.

So I said, 'Grenville, it's no good. You'll never talk to Alston here.'

'He's deaf and cursing the world, I suppose,' laughed Henry Grenville; 'but that makes no difference to me. I could burn out the pack of you, if it weren't that you have the girl with you.'

'You know that, too?' said I.

'Yes, I know about everything, Willis.'

'There's one thing you don't know,' said I. 'And that is that Alston and Daggett and the girl are not here now.'

'Not there now?'

'I came back here to hold you fellows for a while; and I think I've done it long enough, Grenville.'

The minute I named the idea, they seemed to see the point of it. There was a general shout of rage and disappointment, and I could hear them making for their horses again. But then Grenville began to shout:

'Stay where you are! Stay where you are, everybody! We've missed the rest of them by this time. Do you think that Doc Willis would show the cards before their game was won? But I tell you it's not won for them, by a long shot, if we can get Willis into our hands! Let us land Willis, and we'll have the others pretty much when we please!'

That sounded very like sense to me. In the whole crowd, Zack and Roger Beckett were not much use at fighting. That left Alston and Buck Logan to bear the brunt of the attack, and I didn't think they would have any very great luck in managing to hold off Grenville and his men.

However, here was Grenville sending his fellows back to their posts. The shadows were gathering pretty thick and fast.

He called, 'Well, are you ready to come out, Willis?'

'What sort of a deal will you make with me?' I answered him.

He replied in a way that nearly took my breath. 'You come with us, and I'll make you pretty good terms!'

Generous? Why, it was almost foolish. Here I was out of the picture, and all he had to do was to wait for his time to put a chunk of lead through me. But instead of that, he offered to take me on his crew as though I was a free man and had never done him a stroke of harm.

I said, 'Will you let me come and talk with you on that?'

'Come out as free as you please,' said Grenville.

'Show yourself first,' said I. 'Some of your gents ain't very friendly to me, and they might use the chance to shoot from behind.'

'Here I am,' says Grenville, and he stepped out into the open, as brave as ever he was. There was nothing of the yaller streak in that Grenville.

So I got up, in my turn, and walked out of the brush. I said, 'I've come out here to talk to you, Grenville, because you're terribly white, it seems to me. But the first thing I got to say to you is that I can't go to work for you. I can't switch hosses in the middle of the stream.'

'Is that final?'

'It is,' says I.

'Well,' said Grenville, 'just tell me, if you please, what you expect me to do with you?'

'You're the boss,' said I, 'I'd suggest something like this: They got your brother. And you got me. See if they won't arrange a trade for him?'

'They have Larry!' shouted Grenville.

'Why man,' said I, 'didn't you know that?'

He only groaned, 'Is it true, Willis?'

'It's true.'

'If they do him a harm,' said Grenville, 'I'll flay them alive.'

Then he said, looking pretty sick and weak, 'I never should have let him come. Think of a lad like that, blasting a fine life, with a sordid adventure—'

He broke off and snapped at me, 'What happened?'

'About Larry?'

'Yes.'

'He took a pot shot at me this morning, and my hoss Jupe got his head between the rifle and me. Jupe died, and I hit the ground alive. Afterward I got up behind Larry. Him and me had a little mix. And I persuaded him to come along with me, real friendly.'

'Darn it, Willis!' said he. 'You were born to ruin my plans. Is the boy hurt?'

'Not a scratch.'

'And yet you had him under after he'd killed

your horse?'

'That was it.'

He rubbed his hard knuckles across his chin and stared at me. 'All right, Doc,' said he. 'I'd like to turn you loose and let you go on your way for this; but before I can do that I've got to try my hand at getting my brother loose from Alston, and – Buck Logan.'

He hesitated a little before he used that name, which made me suspect that he thought the opposition to the scheme would come from Buck alone.

'You persuade Alston,' said I; 'and I'll swear that Buck will do what he can to get me back.'

'Do you think so?' smiled Grenville. 'Well, son, let me tell you this: They know that while they have my brother, they have a weapon that will keep me from bothering them a mite. If they can get the stuff they're after, they can walk right out of the valley with it; and I'll never be able to raise a hand at them, because they know that Larry means a lot more to me than all the money in the world. You understand? Now, Doc, you've had a chance to size up both Buck and Alston. Tell me frankly. Do you really think that either of them would prefer your safety to a fair chance to get away with the loot?'

I thought it over, and a lot of black thoughts swarmed up into my mind.

'About Alston I know,' said I. 'He'd never turn his hand to do me a good turn, or anybody else, except one.'

'Meaning the girl,' said Grenville.

'You seem pretty well informed,' I couldn't help saying to him.

'Why, Willis,' said he, 'I know enough about that crew to be sick of them. But I could tell Alston, if I had the chance, that the girl is not for him. She has too much sense. He thinks he can buy her; but he can't – not in one short life!'

That pleased me a good deal.

'What do you know about her?' said I.

He squinted at me and then smiled. 'Has she hit you, too?' said Grenville. 'Well, she has a way about her, I admit. No doubt about that. But she's made quick work with you. Well, I know enough about her to respect her, if that's what you mean. But what you say about Buck Logan interests me a lot. Do you really think that he would put a high value on you, old-timer?'

'Do you think I'm wrong?' said I.

'You can see that I think that. But we'll see who's right in the long run. We'll not have far to run, at that. We'll go up there to the house and propose a dicker. A trade of you for my brother, and if Logan is the white man you think he is, he'll certainly see that the trade is made, rather than leave you in our hands. Isn't that right?'

I admitted that it was.

And so, in another five minutes I found myself sitting behind Grenville on his horse. He hadn't asked me to give my word that I wouldn't try to escape on the way. He didn't have to, because the rest of the gang were riding along behind us; and I would as soon have jumped into the fire as tried to get away under the guns of that lot.

I studied them in the evening light, and I'll tell you they were a hardy lot.

'Where did you get these thugs?' I asked Grenville.

'The finest lot of cutthroats out of jail,' he chuckled; 'but they'll serve their purpose. Here we are, old-timer. Now we'll see what happens with your friend in the Daggett house.'

XV

Enemies Bargain

We came upon the house from behind one of the nearest trees in the edge of the clearing that surrounded the old place. Grenville started shouting; and, in a few seconds, a window was thrown up by some one who took care to keep out of sight of us.

The voice of Buck Logan called out: 'Hello, Grenville!'

'It's Grenville,' answered Henry Grenville. 'I've come to talk business.'

'Old son,' said Buck, and his voice was that of a gent who is pretty well pleased with himself, 'tell me what you got to say.'

'I've come to show you how generous I can be,' said Grenville. 'If you wish to listen!'

'Fire away.'

'I have some property that belongs to your side of the fence,' said Grenville.

'Have you?'

'You can guess what that property is.'

'You mean Doc Willis, I suppose?'

'That's what I mean.'

Buck Logan laughed; and, as the big sound of his laughter come floating out to me, it made me wince, I can tell you.

Grenville looked aside at me. 'How does that sound to you?' he asked.

'Wait a minute,' said I. 'The party ain't over yet. We'll do the voting at the end of it.'

'Just as you say. Listen!'

There was the big throat of Buck Logan bellowing:

'I hear what you have to say, Grenville. I never thought much of you as a business man, but I do now. You want to drive a bargain, do you?'

'That's what I'm here for.'

'And you know that we have something that belongs to you, too? You know that, Grenville?'

'You have,' admitted Grenville.

'Do you aim to say that the two parties should be exchanged?'

'Why not?' said Grenville. 'That kid brother of mine is no hand with a gun, and Willis is your fighting ace.'

'You've told one lie,' I said in an undertone. 'That brother of yours shoots straight enough to satisfy me.'

'I like the way you talk up,' said Buck, 'but I've got to say that you're looking at this thing pretty crooked, old-timer. I'd like nothing better than to make a friendly deal with you, but you got to look at it this way – so long as I have your brother, I've got you in my pocket. I'll have no trouble with you so long as I have him.' And he broke out with his laughter again.

It brought a growl from Grenville. 'Willis is thanking you for what you have to say,' he cut in.

I could hear Buck Logan suddenly begin to swear in a deep rumble. 'Is Willis there with you?' he asked.

'Willis is here,' said Grenville.

'Hello, Doc,' called Logan.

'Hello,' said I, pretty feeble.

'Are you well, old man?'

'I'm well enough,' said I.

'Mind you,' said Buck. 'Grenville is a white man; and I know that you're in no danger with him. Otherwise I'd cut off an arm to have you clean away from him.'

I didn't make any answer. It was pretty thin talk, after what I had stood there and heard him saying just before.

'You there still, Doc?' called Buck, pretty anxious.

'Oh, I'm here,' said I. 'And I'm listening. Have you got any more to say?'

'Lots more! Lots more!' said Buck Logan. 'And in the first place—'

'We've heard enough,' said Grenville. 'I brought Doc here mostly to let him see what a hound you are, Logan; and, if I am not mistaken, I'll have him lined up against you before the morning!'

'Line him up! Line him up!' shouted Logan. 'Line up a hundred more like him. Welcome to them, old-timer. But what I want you to notice is that I'll still have your brother Larry along with me; and while I have him, I'm not worrying, Grenville.' He broke off, laughing again.

Grenville swore softly, under his breath. He called out, 'I'm going off, Logan; but I expect you'll come to your senses after a time. You may think that I put a higher value on my brother than the case is; but you may be wrong – never forget that. And if you're wrong, with Doc Willis on my side, I can eat the rest of you alive, Logan! You hear me?'

'Good!' said Logan. 'It'd be a fine meal. Especially considering what we'll have in our pockets before long. So long, old-timer! Keep a watch on this house; and, if I change my mind, I'll show you a pair of lights in this window.'

'I hear you,' said Grenville, 'So long!'

He talked cool enough, but he was pretty sick at this sort of talk; and, as he went back through the trees, he hardly had the energy to tell a couple of his men to keep a watch over the house.

Then he walked on with me; and he said: 'You've heard, Doc?'

'I heard,' I admitted.

'And what do you think?'

'I'm not thinking!' said I.

'Come!' said he. 'You have to confess that I was a

good prophet. I told you what would happen, and what I said has turned out to be true. Is that right?'

I admitted that it was right, and I had to admit it with a groan.

'I treated him white, Grenville,' I explained, to let him know why I was so badly cut up.

'Of course you did – and you treat most people white, perhaps too white for your own good. If you had aimed to kill when we came up with you back there in the wood, perhaps you would be inside that house, yonder; and we would be burying our dead back in the clearing. However, let that go. I have two things to say. The first is the least important. It is that I still want you with me, and that I'll pay you five thousand dollars. The second is that I like you, my friend; and, if you play with me, you'll have a chance to see all of the cards laid upon the table face up.'

'Right,' said I. 'I like what you say fine. And I dunno what it is that holds me back. It ain't that I care what people will say about me. I've had myself damned in about every known way, a long time before this. But, as a matter of fact, I don't think that I can go in with you, Grenville.'

'You're sure?'

'I suppose I am.'

'Will you give me one good reason?'

'I'll try to.'

'You can't doubt that those fellows in there are all thugs.'

'Daggett?' said I.

'Daggett?' said he, and his face and his voice softened a lot. 'That poor old man! I'm sorry to know that he's in their hands, because he'll get no good out of it, whatever they may find in the house!'

'No good at all?'

'From those stone-hearted devils? I should say not!'

I shook my head. It was pretty hard talk, but I was beginning to feel that Grenville was as right as the fellows in that house were wrong.

He went on, 'What I want you to see for yourself is that if they will treat you badly now, they would plan to treat you badly even if you were with them, working heart and soul for them. Doesn't that stand to reason?'

I had to admit that there was a good deal in what he had to say; and he added, 'Oh, I know them and I hate them as much as you'll come to hate them before you're done with them.'

Then he made a pause and broke in, 'Give me your answer, Doc.'

I said: 'I'd like to do it, but I started in this game with Logan and his crew inside of that house. They've never cut me off of their list. And I've got no more from them and this game than I might of expected from anybody that I was working for – unless he was my friend. And I think that I'll have to stick by them, Grenville.'

'Ah, well,' said he, 'I'll change your mind for you before the morning. I've got to. Because if they have Larry, I've got to have something on my side of the fence to play off against that power – and what can it be except you? What can it be?'

Just then there was a call from the trees toward the house:

'Hey, chief, they've started in showing two lights from that window–'

I could hardly believe it, and Grenville shouted with his surprise; but, when we ran back through the woods and came to the spot, we saw that he had told us right. There was the two lights burning from the window where Logan said he would show them if he decided he must change his mind.

And they looked mighty good to me, I can tell you.

XVI

Lou Demands Fair Play

Grenville seemed hardly able to believe his eyes. And he kept saying over and over, 'I can't make it out. For Logan or Alston to do a thing like this! I can't make it out.'

Well, for my part, I thought that when they had had a chance to consider everything, they had decided that it would be better not to leave me in the lurch; and so they had changed their minds.

There wasn't much of a dicker. Grenville just called out to make out what the meaning of the two lights in the window might be, and the answer came right back that it was what I wished for – Larry Grenville was to be turned over for me in a fair exchange. Out came Larry Grenville, walking straight down the path of the lamplight, and into the same path I walked freely toward the house. We met in the center, and Larry held out his hand.

'I thought I was done for in that fine gang of

thugs, old-timer. I'm glad you were out there to make the exchange, but will you tell me one thing?'

'I'd like to if I can, Larry.'

'How the devil did you ever hook up with such a low crowd?'

He didn't mean to be sassy. He was just speaking his mind out – and that was no great compliment to Alston, big Buck Logan, and the rest.

'They may look low to you,' I told him, 'and they may be low; but they're the crowd that I'm playing this game with, and they'll have to do for me.' I could not help saying, 'This here business is apt to turn into a fight, before long. And I give you one word of advice, keep clear of me, Larry, because you've used up your share of luck with me. But tell me one thing, what made them change their minds about making the exchange?'

'Can't you guess, you lucky dog?' asked Larry Grenville. 'Why, it was the girl, of course. She just put down her foot and said she wouldn't take a step in the direction they wanted her to go until she saw you back in the house.'

Take it all in all, I think that was about the best news I had ever heard.

'Thanks, Larry,' said I. 'I sure appreciate you telling me this.'

He grinned at me in rather a crooked fashion. 'It's all right, Doc,' said he. 'I was a loser with her before I ever had a chance to be a winner. So long.'

He held out his hand. I took it with a good, hard grip, and then he passed on toward the woods, and

I went on toward the Daggett house.

When I got to the door, there was Alston, opening it for me, and giving me a sort of a dark, sour, upward glance. He met me in silence; and I passed him and went on into the house, hating him with all my heart, I can tell you. Right back there in the hall I met Buck, and there was a good deal of difference. He came straight up to me and stretched out his big bear paw of a hand.

'Why, old-timer,' said he, 'dog-gone me if it ain't good to see you back here with us.'

I looked Buck straight in the eye and tried to read something behind his big, ugly face. But all I could see there seemed like honesty, to me. Every time I came near him, lately, he had seemed more and more like a puzzle to me; and now I said:

'Look here, Buck. I stood out yonder under the trees and listened to the talk you made with Grenville. What was I to make of that?'

'What were you to make of it?' said Buck. 'Why, simply this – that I know Henry Grenville is a white man, and that you were in no danger with him.'

'That sounds reasonable, Buck,' said I; 'but the fact is that while I was listening to you, it seemed to me that you didn't give a darn whether you ever seen me again. But beyond all that is the fact that while Grenville is a white man, right enough, he has a lot of thugs with him that hate my heart and that would plant me full of lead, if they had more than half a chance.'

'Don't tell me that, Doc!' says Buck. 'Don't tell me

that, old boy!'

'You didn't know it?'

'Know it? Of course not!'

I stared at him, trying to make out whether he was joking, or whether he was really in earnest. He seemed in earnest, and there was nothing I could do to get at the real truth in him. If he wanted to deceive me, there was no doubt that he could do it. I was no match for that smooth-talking way that he had with him. He was altogether too deep for me.

I asked after Daggett, then; and Buck told me that Daggett had been in a terrible state by the time they got him to the house, and that he had been so nervous and cut up that they had put him to bed and quieted him down with an opium pill that Alston had.

'Old Daggett is pretty far spent,' said Buck; 'but he knew his house. He's pretty far gone; but, still, he knew his house. And that was one thing! However, I don't think he'll stay long in this here house. Not very long! And not long in this life, either, Doc, if I'm not mistaken.'

I agreed with that. Because anybody with half an eye could see that the poor old fellow was about two thirds dead.

Then I asked if I could see Lou Wilson.

He dropped his head a little and frowned, very thoughtful.

I snapped out, 'Tell me straight. Are you afraid for me to see the girl?'

'No, I'm not afraid,' said he.

But no matter what his words were, I knew that he meant something different. He was afraid. He was mighty afraid. Well, I could see him thinking the thing over, pretty careful, and then he said:

'Go ahead. You see Lou and talk with her. Only – you won't try to mix into her business and ours, too much?'

He looked at me with a frown, and I could see that he was on the edge of saying something more. But he checked himself and he only remarked, 'Well, you go ahead and see her. She's upstairs. The first room on the right.'

So I went up the stairs, thinking things over slowly; and, when I got to the first room on the right, I tapped at the door.

'Come in!' sang out the voice of Lou.

I opened the door and went in. And there was Lou standing in front of a mirror with her fine hair streaming down her back – but that hair which had been a fine brown during the day, was a bright, shining red at night!

XVII

The Plot Begins to Work

I don't mean that that was the only change. Her face was changed, too. There was a deep blue look about the eyes that had been gray in the daytime – gray and sky-blue, if you know what I mean. But here at night there was nothing about them except the deep violet blue that the eyes of beautiful women sometimes have.

I had never noticed her eyelashes particular before in the daytime; but now, though it was only the night, I could see them perfectly clear and fine, and that was a great surprise to me. They were jet black, and long.

But that wasn't all. No, even her skin had changed. It had been a fine, healthy-looking sort of a brownish skin before – an olive skin, if anything. But now it was very different, it was all pink and white. It was the sort of a skin that an eleven-year-old girl has before the sun has begun to roughen her up, and change her a lot, and make her wrinkled around the eyes. No, sir, she was so different that you wouldn't believe it; and that neck and throat of hers, that had been almost as brown as an Indian's, was now as snow and polished-up looking as a queen's might have been.

I was a good deal surprised, of course; and I hung there in the doorway and stared like a fool.

'Confound it!' says Lou; and she stamps on the floor. 'Confound it, how was I to remember that you were back in the crowd again!'

I could see that she would not have cared if any of the others had popped in to see her, but I was different. I didn't know whether to be flattered or just sad.

I said, 'Look here, Lou, what's wrong with you and your hair? Or are you Lou Wilson!'

'I'm her twin sister,' says Lou. 'I'm the red-haired, blue-eyed kid; and don't you forget it!'

Well, it was her voice. She might change the rest of herself, complete as a picture painted over; but she couldn't change that husky voice. It was Lou, right enough.

'What's happened?' says I.

'I tumbled in a stack of paints,' says Lou; 'that's all. Does it bother you a lot, old-timer?'

I couldn't speak, for a minute.

'Do I look like the devil?' says Lou.

'Nearly,' says I.

She took up a mirror and squinted at herself.

'Why,' says she, 'the way it looks to me, I'm very

nearly beautiful, in this rig.'

Says I, 'Lou, you take it from me. You was never meant to be beautiful.'

She dropped the mirror and swung around at me. 'Say, Doc, how do you get that way?' she snapped. 'Am I as homely as all that?'

'I don't mean homely,' said I; 'but the fact is, Lou, that you –'

'Never mind,' says she. 'Don't explain. When I want to get the truth, I'll come to you. When I want to be happy, I'll go to somebody else.'

Well, that was a good deal of a settler for me, as you can see for yourself; but at the same time, I wasn't finished.

'What's it all going to be about?' I asked her.

But just then a pair of voices floated up toward us through the open window and Lou didn't answer. It was old man Daggett, and Buck Logan was there walking along with him.

We heard Daggett saying, 'In the morning I shall take you for a ride up and down the valley, as far as we can go.'

'The whole length of it, Mr. Daggett?' says Buck, very respectful. 'Will we have time for that in one day?'

Daggett laughed a little. 'You wouldn't think there was time, my friend Logan, looking at those trees. But let me tell you that the good road by which you come into the valley is continued up and down the entire length of it. I had it cut out; and I built the little bridges over every creek and gully, so that one can ride at a hot pace through the entire length and breadth of Daggett Valley –'

He added quickly, 'Excuse me for giving it that name. But about a year ago, you understand, some of the miners who had struck it rich here, began to call the valley after my name; and it's become rather a habit here.'

That took my breath, but I could see what had happened. Poor old Daggett had been snatched back to the old days, that long, long time ago, when Daggett Valley was still packed with miners, and when he had been the king of the place, looked up to, and worshipped, and respected a lot by everybody. Yes, he was back in those old days, and he was taking Buck Logan around and treating him like a guest, and trying to make him happy.

Somehow that gave me a sort of a tear in the eye, to hear Daggett talk like that. You could see in a flash just what sort of a fellow he had been in those old days, mighty generous, trying to make other folks happy, free and easy, proud of his fortune, and wanting to show it off to other folks.

'It'll be a fine trip,' Buck Logan was saying. 'It'll be fine to go with you, Mr. Daggett!'

'It will be my privilege –' said the old man; and then he stopped. For he had caught the sound of Lou's voice, she having exclaimed something about old man Daggett reliving the past.

'No,' said old Daggett. 'That was not my wife. Her voice is pitched high, and very light. It must be one of the servants.'

'I been sort of wondering,' says Buck Logan, 'how Mrs. Daggett would get on out here in the wilderness, as you might call it.'

'Ah! Ah!' says old Daggett. 'Do you think it will be hard for a lady to be happy out here?'

'No, no,' answered Buck. 'That wasn't what I meant to say. Sure she could be happy here. Look at a fine, big house like this – why, any woman would be pretty proud and glad to live in it, I should say.'

'I think so, too,' said Daggett, pretty self-satisfied. 'I think so, too! Why couldn't she be happy here? A little restless at first, perhaps! A little restless at first! But soon the beauty of the forest would begin to work on her mind –'

He was getting pretty excited.

'There ain't any doubt that you're right,' said Buck Logan. 'Besides,' he added in a sort of a leading voice, 'sometimes it's a good thing to get folks away from the city – a lot of bad things in the cities, bad for the men and bad for the women.'

He said that with just a little weight on the last word, and I wondered that he dared to; but Daggett broke out with a groan, 'Ah, Logan, that is true! That is bitterly true, of course! But here in the wilderness, a man can forget his past. And a woman can forget hers. Is not that true?'

'Nothing truer was ever said,' remarked Buck Logan.

Well, that was enough explanation for the crazy thing that old Daggett had done in building this house away out here in the wilderness. It was something about his wife – no freak of his own, but a thing that he had done for her sake. And I couldn't help pitying him more than ever, for he seemed almost tragic.

But I couldn't fit everything together. I couldn't make out the murder that he accused himself of. There were a thousand blanks in the true story that lived around the memory of the Daggett house. And, as I stood there in the night, I wondered how long it would be before I got at the truth. Or would I ever? I was a lot closer to the time than I guessed. And before the morning came I was to know everything that could be told of Daggett, and his poor wife, and Alston – yes, and of Carberry, too.

Well, just then the voice of Alston sang out, 'Hello, Buck, are you there?'

'Here I am,' says Buck.

'It's about time,' says Alston.

'All right,' says Buck.

'By Heaven!' gasped Daggett. 'Whose voice is that?'

'Why do you ask?' said Buck.

'Because it sounded to me – no, it can't be – but it sounded to me like the voice of that archdevil, Alston!'

XVIII

The Stage is Set

What a chill it sent through me to hear that! There was a man and a voice that Daggett had been traveling with for days and days, and suddenly he recognized it like a flash. But I suppose that being brought back to the old place had cleared up his brain. Not all of it – he was still a long distance from the normal. But he had recovered enough to have bright spots as well as the darkness; and so it was that he recognized the voice of Alston – not out of the present, but out of the past of those long years ago.

There was electricity in the air, I can tell you. Right then I had the sense of a tragedy that was to come.

Buck took Daggett back into the house; and, as I watched him go, I wondered if the old man wasn't like a bull taken to the slaughter. I wondered if he'd ever come out again, alive.

After a minute, out came Buck; and I heard his voice calling softly, 'Doc! Oh, Doc Willis!'

I looked at Lou, and she nodded her head for me to go.

I sneaked out, and then I waited until he called again. After that, I answered him; and I went out, because I didn't want him to think that maybe I had been overhearing what had been said between him and Daggett.

'You're here, eh?' said Buck.

'Yes.'

'Have you seen old Daggett, lately?'

'No,' said I. 'Is he missing?'

'Not missing,' said Buck; 'but I wondered – well, let it go.'

Of course he was hinting that perhaps I had overheard the conversation, but he thought that perhaps it wasn't important enough to emphasize.

He said, 'There hasn't been a sound from the woods, eh?'

'No,' said I, 'there hasn't.'

'Seems strange,' said Buck Logan, 'that Grenville should lie out there so quiet in spite of all the men he has with him. Don't it seem strange to you?'

'Yes,' I admitted, 'it sure does.'

'What do you think he could have up his sleeve?'

'No idea in the world!'

'He's planning some sort of trouble – some sort of real trouble for us,' said Buck; 'you can depend on that. He isn't the sort of fellow who would waste his time.'

'I suppose not,' said I.

'But you're keeping watch for us?' said Buck, quick and sharp.

'Am I the only one to keep up that job?' said I.

'Not the only one, of course,' said Buck; 'we're all keeping an eye peeled. But Zack and Roger Beckett, they ain't of much use, as you know; and me and Alston have Daggett on our hands.'

'Sure,' said I.

'Is there anything special up to-night?'

'Special? To-night?' said Buck, and cleared his throat. 'No, not to-night. The only reason I came out here was to tell you that we appreciate you, Doc. Also, I wanted to ask you to keep a sharp lookout now that we have the girl and Daggett here along with us.'

'Sure,' I said. 'I understand. This here Grenville has been holding back and taking things easy, hoping that when the time comes he would be able to scoop up Daggett and the girl, either coming into the valley or after they got here. Ain't that right?'

'Exactly, Doc. Exactly.'

'And now that the two of them are here, Grenville is going to cut loose pretty soon.'

'Yes,' said Buck, 'and you never can tell when. A slippery devil, that chap Grenville is. Got a brain in his head that's working all the time, and you won't forget it.'

'I won't forget it,' I told Buck.

'And you'll stay busy on the job?'

'I will.'

'I'll shake with you on that,' said Buck.

Well, I took his hand in the dark, and then he started back towards the house. He strolled along; and he even whistled a note or two of a song; and then he went inside. By that time I was standing on a needle edge; for I was beginning to expect things to happen. There was a lot of reasons for what I expected to happen.

In the first place, there was no occasion why Buck should of made a point of looking me up there in the night except for a very definite purpose. And that was what he might want to make sure that he had got me outside of the house – important because of something that him and Alston wanted to do inside of it.

So I made up my mind to a number of things. I decided that right on this first night Alston and Logan were going to try to make their big play. And I decided, in addition to that, that they was going to try to make it right away.

But what was I to do? I couldn't guess what they would be about. I knew that it must have something to do with the make-up that the girl was wearing, but just what Lou was to be used for beat me complete.

Well, I looked over the house and I could see several windows lighted. One was the dining room. And one was the room of the old man Daggett, to the front of the house.

I turned the corner of the place; and there I seen

another lighted window, one that opened out onto a little balcony, built strong and snug against the side of the house.

I decided right there that I would have to take a look, because I had to do something; and, guessing as much as I guessed, I would of gone plumb mad if I had had to stand around and look at the stars when robbery – murder – I didn't know what all – might be taking place in the Daggett house.

The side of the house was pretty easy to climb on account of the big supports of the balcony that run down right to the ground. I climbed up, taking care not to make no sound at all, and I honestly think that nobody standing right under me could of heard a whisper from my work.

A good thing that I was so silent, too, because when I got to the outer edge of the balcony and lifted up, I seen that a man had reached the balcony ahead of me.

However, the important thing was not what was outside the window. It was what was inside the window. And that was about the queerest picture I had ever seen before – queerer, I'd make a guess, than you have ever seen, either.

There was a table right in the center of the space that I looked into through the window, and up to this table there was two chairs drawn. And in one chair sat Lou, but fixed up so you would never of knowed her.

Of course you can guess that she was made up the way I had seen her not a little while before, but that wasn't all. Her face was changed, then, but her clothes was changed now. She wore a big, broad, black hat, with a black feather curling down one side of it, and the brim looped up on the other side, like the pictures of riding hats you used to see in some of the old-fashioned books. And she had on a tailored suit; and around her neck there was a big brown fur, that looked like real fox, and mighty expensive. She had on a pair of black kid gloves, long and fancy looking; I mean to say that she had one of those gloves on, but the other glove was off and held in the covered hand. And the hand that was bare, why, it shone like anything. So that you wouldn't believe it! On one of the fingers of it there was a diamond that sparkled and glittered something wonderful to see. Yes, she had used up a considerable deal of whiting on those brown hands of her.

On the far side of the table from her there was a gent that I didn't know, at first. He wore longish black hair, and he had straight black-eyebrows that give him a sort of devilish look. And he was smooth shaven. He wore a black coat, padded out on the shoulders, the way coats used to be worn, a long time ago.

But in a minute this fellow smiled; and, by something in his smile, I knew him. Perhaps you've guessed already – yes, it was Alston! It was Alston, with his mean smile; but his gray beard was gone, which showed a good chin, and a straight, cruel, cunning mouth. He had covered up his gray hair with a longish black wig, with the hair of it brushed back a good deal, giving him a sort of an artistic look. And he wore a black silk cravat with a big diamond pin stuck into it – big enough and shining enough to stop a train with, I can tell you!

But I haven't told you all. I'll tell you that on the table between the two of them there was a smooth gray chamois bag, all crumpled up; and, spilled out of the mouth of the bag, there was a whole double handful of jewels.

By this time my slow brain was beginning to translate what I was seeing into the facts of the case. I knew, now, that this was a real effort to reproduce something that had been in this same room a long time before. But what could that be?

Pretty soon, Alston says, 'Hush, Lou! What was that?'

'Somebody walking up the stairs,' she answered him.

'Aye,' said Alston, after listening for a moment. 'But is it time? No, not for ten minutes, according to what Carberry promised.'

'Carberry?' gasped Lou, looking white even under her make-up.

'Why not Carberry?' said Alston. 'He won't eat you.'

'Carberry! The murderer!' says Lou.

'Darn it,' said Alston, 'I suppose I shouldn't of used that word. But I tell you, you'll never see Carberry's face – no matter how deep he may be in this thing.'

'Ah,' said Lou, with a quick glance over her shoulder toward the window; 'I feel as if somebody was sneaking up behind me with a knife in his hand. Carberry!'

She was hard hit, and no wonder, considering the reputation Carberry wore around those parts of the world.

'Get ready!' said Alston. 'Because I think they're surely coming!'

'What'll I do?'

'Lean back in your chair; and, with your ungloved hand, grab at the jewels. You see?'

'Jewels?' said she, with a grin.

'Well, they look close enough to the real thing. I had this stuff made one at a time, to look like the real things; and I don't think I missed out, very far. He'll never know the difference unless he's seeing clearer than I think the poor old goat can do to-day. He's too upset to notice any of the details, I think. Lean back in your chair – so!'

She leaned back and grabbed at the jewels with one hand, just as he had said; and then Alston said, 'I've got to lean over you now and pretend to be kissing you. You understand, Lou?'

'Did his wife do that?' said Lou.

'Why, she lost her head when she saw that there was a chance to get away from this place – worked out like a story. She spends all his money. Poor Daggett comes West to try to recoup. And he does, because he hits gold, with regular beginner's luck. After he's raked in a lot of the yellow stuff he thinks that he'll bring his wife West and keep her safely here away from all temptation to run up big bills and flirt with the boys. A wild man's notion! She would have gone mad in this place.

'And if it hadn't been for that, she would never have looked at –' He stopped himself.

'Never have looked as low as a gambler?' said Lou.

'Confound your sharp tongue!' says Alston. 'No matter. The main thing was that he walked in and found us – Listen! They are coming toward this place!'

'Yes, right up the stairs –'

'And now down the hall! Hold this position, Lou; you hear me?'

He took her in his arms and put his face close to hers; and I think he would have made it more than just a pretense if she hadn't said, 'If you really kiss me, Al, I'll sink a knife in you. You hear me?'

'You spitfire! You little devil!' he whispered through his teeth. 'It would be almost worth it! Steady – don't tremble! That might give everything away. I'm the one who runs through the danger – not you!'

'Very well,' said Lou. 'I won't throw the game away, now that we've played it this far.'

'Hush!'

I could hear the pair of feet stop outside the door – though they had been apparently trying to move very soft and easy. And in that minute I remember that my heart nearly stopped beating;

and yet I had a chance to think of two things – the fierce, bright eyes of Lou, looking up to Alston, and the shadowy head of the gent outside the window.

Could that shadowy head be Carberry? I wondered.

And then the door opened!

XIX

Seen from the Balcony

Outside the door stood Daggett, looking almost as small as a boy in comparison with the figure of the giant behind him. I thought that that shadow of a man behind must be Buck Logan; but just then he side-stepped back out of view, and I couldn't make sure. Daggett, I expected, would shout or make a start. But he didn't. He just walked into that room with a sort of a puzzled frown on his face, like a man who isn't quite sure of what he's seeing; and then he rubbed his knuckles across his forehead.

He leaned a hand against the wall. 'Good God!' says Daggett. 'This is what I saw in my dream!'

When he spoke, Alston jumped up and away, as though in surprise; and, as he jumped away, Lou leaned forward and covered her face with her hands, shuddering with real fear.

'Alston,' said Daggett, 'I knew I should find you here. Don't ask me how. God showed this thing to me, and I knew it must be!'

'God or the devil!' says Alston. 'Stand away from that door, Daggett; or I'll do you harm.'

'Are you running away?' says Daggett. 'And are you leaving your woman behind you?'

Lou gave a twist and a sort of a moan. Alston backed into a corner of the room, with his right hand always behind him and in his hip pocket. I never saw a man do any better acting.

'Daggett,' says he, 'you're wrong. She's not mine. Only – just now –'

'Just now you planned to run away with this? Is that all? And she is wearing a hat – by accident, I suppose?'

He stepped to the side and looked at her. 'And a riding skirt, too!' said he.

'Curse it, man,' said Alston, 'I want to explain –'

'Hush!' says Daggett, very grand. 'Hush, Alston! Don't you suppose I understand perfectly? I understand everything. And the reason you wanted me to put more and more money into jewels, Martha, I understand that, too. There's only one thing that rather bothers me – not more than a third of those fine fellows are mine! And where did you get the others? Where did you get the others, Alston – or should I ask that question of you, my dear wife?'

You could see that he was holding himself back with a hand of iron, but all the time I kept waiting for that iron hand to snap.

Alston glared at Daggett, and then at Lou; but

Lou did not stir. And Daggett picked up a big ruby – a monster and a sparkler.

'Here's a beauty,' said he, 'that must have cost a good many tens of thousands. I know a bit about the prices of rubies, now; and I wonder how much this thing cost. More than a hundred thousand, I should say. A hundred thousand in one sparkler! Ah, Martha, you and Alston truly have high stakes on the table! Very high! Very high!'

He looked across at Alston and tried to smile, but it was a terrible poor excuse for a smile that he worked up.

'More of them, too,' says he, 'a great many more! Why, Martha, you've let yourself in for your share of a very tidy fortune, here. A great deal more than I could offer you at present, it seems! A great deal more!'

His smooth voice wobbled a bit, here; and his hand went up to his wrinkled old throat.

He went on, 'I see no good reason why I should not take these jewels and the rest, which belong to me, and try to ascertain if they may not have been stolen – as mine were about to be. Do you think of any good reason to advance against this, Alston?' And he scooped the stuff all together and raked it into the chamois bag.

'Will you look at me, Martha?' said he. 'Poor girl, are you really going to give up everything and go off with a rascally gambler like Alston? Alston of all the men in the world! How will you be considered in the East, after this is known? You should know –

because that world means a great deal more to you than it could ever mean to me.'

He put the chamois bag into his pocket; and, as he did that, Alston barked at him, 'Daggett, drop that bag on the table, do you hear me? Put it back where you found it!'

'You speak harshly,' said Daggett, looking more at his 'wife' than at Alston.

'I mean business,' said Alston. 'Your own stuff you may take out, but the rest has no concern of yours attached to it!'

'How can I be sure of that?' said Daggett, gravely. 'I tell you that the property of every honest man is the concern of every other honest man. And how can I tell that these sparklers really belong to you – and to Martha?'

'No other person has claimed them,' said Alston.

'I claim them, then,' said Daggett, 'until the law decides otherwise!'

'Daggett!' barked Alston, raising his voice sharp and hard.

'Don't do it!' said Daggett, shaking his head in a sort of a sad fashion. 'Don't bring out your gun, Alston. I warn you that this evening I am armed. And the truth of what will happen here is revealed to me – I cannot say by what marvelous foresight. But if you draw your weapon I shall shoot you through the head and leave you dead on this floor – stretched beside the table, there. I have seen it all in a vision, Alston, and the very manner of your fall. I beg you in the name of Heaven, believe what

I am telling you. You have planned too much harm against me already, and you are given into my hands now. Will you believe me, Alston?'

Alston, backed into the farthest corner of the room, swayed a little from side to side; and it was wonderful to see the way he made fear and shame and a pretended desire for those faked jewels fight in his face. But finally he said:

'Well, let it go. I only want you to realize, Daggett, that you are changing parts with me, and becoming the real robber where I was only trying to be a robber. And what the law will say to you –'

'I shall be very willing to meet the law face to face,' said Daggett, 'quite as willing – or perhaps a little more so – than you can be. But –'

He broke off, 'I have warned you, Alston. Beware of me!'

'Curse you and your warnings!' said Alston. 'And take this!'

He snatched out a revolver and fired, and I saw Daggett swing his old head to the side and drag out the old revolver that I had seen before. While he swung it up, there was time for a handy man like Alston to of fired again half a dozen times. I was about to break through and stop the slaughter, when all at once I remembered that this was only an acted scene – acted by everybody except old Daggett. He was in the deadest sort of earnest. He brought his old gun down on the mark and fired.

Alston let his Colt drop with a clatter to the floor, and he clasped his hands over his head and staggered forward. He pitched on his face beside the table and twisted over on his back and lay still in a sprawling shape, with a great smear of red down his face and through his hair; and in his hand I could see the little red sponge with which he'd done the trick – in or under his hand, away from the view of Daggett.

As for Daggett, he stood up stiff and straight for a minute, and then dropped the gun into his coat pocket.

'I knew it would happen exactly like this,' he said quietly. 'I knew it with a very strange fore-knowledge. Martha, God have pity on your wretched soul, because you were the cause of this. You were the cause of this –'

All at once there was a heavy knocking at the front of the house. It made my hair stand on end, and it seemed to throw a terrible chill into Daggett. He had been as calm as could be, up to this point; but now he went off the handle in a wild way, throwing his hands above his head. He turned into a child, very pitiful to see.

'Martha! Martha!' says he. 'What shall I do? Oh, what shall I do? Help me, Martha, in Heaven's name! Help me, I pray you!'

She only flung herself out of her chair, without giving a chance to see her face, and kneeled beside Alston.

And I could see Alston's lips move as he said, 'Good, girl! Well done! Well done!'

'You treacherous devil!' groaned Daggett. 'The

whole world is against me, and I have killed a man –'

He turned and plunged from the room just as the knock in the front part of the house was repeated. At the same time, the shadowy shape of a man which had been kneeling in front of the window jumped up and turned around toward me with a grunt of excitement; and I gave him something that I had prepared for him a long time before – the long barrel of my Colt slammed along the side of his head so that I thought that I could feel the skull spring and bend under the shock. He gave one gasp and flopped on his face on the floor of the balcony, just as old Alston, within the room, scrambled to his feet and started to say, 'Honey, you worked it like a fine actress. And now if Carberry –'

Here he heard the gasp from the balcony and turned his head sharply toward us.

'What's that?' he snarled. 'Go and see, Lou. Because if –'

I didn't wait to hear any more. I dropped from my place and shinnied down the pillar and dropped to the ground; and, as I jumped away, a gun spurted fire above me, and a bullet almost tagged my head. It was Alston, standing on the balcony and raging like a madman, because I suppose he saw now that this fine scheme of his, the deepest and the smartest that ever any crook every invented, was now wasted and all gone to pot.

However, I didn't have any chance to stand there

and think these things out. I just ducked around the corner of the house and out of range of that barking gun of his; and, as I ran, I jerked out my own Colt again. A right good thing I did, too!

The Hiding Place

All the devil had broke loose around that house, I can tell you. I heard some one shouting, off in the woods; and then there was the sudden roaring of a pair of guns in the basement of the house; and then the scream of a man in a terrible lot of agony. Dying, I supposed – because the scream ended quick and short and sharp.

I ran straight on, beginning to wish that I was well out of this mess, and wondering how long it would be before Grenville and his gang jumped that house and scooped up everybody that was in it. And just as I got that idea I see a door open in the bottom of the house where I had never knowed that there had been a door before. I seen that door opened, and a man run out into the trees.

Sort of by instinct, I yanked up my gun to be ready for trouble; but this gent he run straight past me, and I seen that it was old Daggett. He had his gun in one hand, and he had the chamois bag in the other; and, though he passed within a few feet of me, he didn't seem to guess that I was there.

He ducked into the trees; but, after he had gone a step or two he stooped, and he jerked up what looked to me like a stone that weighed half a ton. He jerked that stone up and throwed the bag in under it, and then he turned around and he run back to the house and entered in through the side door. And that door closed after him, and there was the side of the house looking just as it had looked before.

The noise had all died down, too. I felt almost as though I had been dreaming these things, and had waked up like a sleepwalker.

The first thing I did was to run to that big-looking stone and lay hold of it. No, it was only a surface slab; and it come up light and easy in my hand. I picked out the chamois bag; but when I did that, my hand touched something else in there. I lighted a match and looked.

It was the rotted shred of something that looked as though it might of been chamois in its day. But it was rotted by dampness and time; and its contents was spilled out onto the gravel; and I seen that there was a collection of jewels like them that had been on the table in the room upstairs just a little time before.

Well, it let in light on my slow head, at last. I seen the thing in one great crash.

In those old days, Alston had come to this house

carrying with him loot that he got by stealing or by gambling. You couldn't hardly tell which. And he had aimed to collect pretty Martha Daggett – just as he had aimed to collect Lou Wilson, this next time. And he had been about to walk away with the girl and the jewels when in steps old Daggett – who maybe had come back early from a journey; and Daggett had spoiled everything. He had shot down Alston, and he had run down through the house.

Nobody knew where he had gone. They took it for granted that he had hidden the loot in the lower part of the old house, and that was the reason they had searched and searched. But why they hadn't simply torn the house to bits in the search was because this treasure was such a dog-gone small handful that nobody could very well hope to find it if the house was turned into debris.

So, finally, the grand scheme had come into the head of Alston when he seen, in Denver, a girl that had the same sort of features that Martha Daggett had.

He had come out here; and he had staged this thing, fixing up the house and getting it all ready so that it would look just the way the place had looked in the old days – or near enough to the way that it had looked to fool a half-witted old man. And then everything was rehearsed just the way it had turned out on that other night – except that this time there was to be a close watch on where Daggett ran, and what he did with the sparklers.

And that was where this here fine scheme had broken down. Perhaps that scream that I had heard in the house explained a part of it. But anyway, the gent or the gents that was to watch where Daggett run had lost out. And only by chance I had come onto the spot where the old man put the loot.

I thought this out in half a dozen seconds, while I was taking up the jewels. And then, as I cupped them in my hand, I wondered who there was in the world that would take them away from me – excepting the part of them that belonged to Daggett, and which I swore should go back into his hands and to nobody else's.

There was other parts of the whole thing that I didn't understand at all. And among the rest of it, I couldn't make out just where Buck Logan fitted in, because he was certainly more than a mere overseer of the work on the house. Neither could I tell where Carberry belonged; and I half suspected that I would never know, because Alston had promised the girl that she would never see the face of the old bandit. Then there was the Grenvilles. How did they come into the picture?

Well, time would take care of all of that, I thought. Then I decided that the first thing I should have to do was to go find Daggett. I wanted to get Lou out of this mess; but I felt somehow that no matter what happened, Lou would be pretty well able to take care of herself. Old Daggett, he was a different matter.

How he had managed to get clear of the house in spite of the rest of them, I couldn't tell. It was beyond me how he had been able to fool old Alston and such a sharp fellow as Buck Logan; but the fact was that nobody had seen him leave the house, and maybe no one had seen him enter it again.

Now, maybe I was wrong, after all; for just as I was about to start toward the house, I saw the same section of the bottom of the wall swing open like a door, and three men came sneaking out. They came slowly up toward the woods, playing a strong light over the ground.

'This is the way he came. No doubt about that. I could swear to these footsteps!' said a voice that I thought I knew.

A moment later, as they came closer, I heard him say again, 'Here he went, running all the way. Who would have thought there was such life in the old chap?'

I recognized the voice for certain this time. It was Henry Grenville.

'Then how come that he turned around and went back into the house?' one of the other two asked.

'Maybe we'll find that out in turn,' said Henry Grenville. 'The first thing is to run down these tracks.'

'What a mess Logan is, eh?' said another of the three. 'Never seen a face like his!'

'And he hollered loud enough!' says another.

'He had reason, poor devil,' said Grenville. 'He

had very good reason. I don't think he'll ever see the light of day again. He's paid for his part in this game!'

'Blind forever!'

'Yes, I had a good look at his eyes. They're ruined.'

That was a shock for me, but hardly as much as the next thing I heard.

'Maybe he deserves what he got,' says one of Grenville's helpers. And Grenville himself answered up quick and sharp, 'Deserves what he got? That devil deserved to be burned alive, inch by inch! There never was such a scoundrel since the world began. Even that Alston is a white man – almost a saint, compared with – Logan!'

Well, I have traveled with Buck, bunked with him, cooked for him, eaten with him, and pretty near done everything except fight with him; and I couldn't see why he come in for any such talk as this, which was pretty sweeping, as you got to admit. But there was no doubt that there must of been something in what Grenville said, because he wasn't the sort of a man to say things rash. He was a man who would have reasons for what he said, and that had a lot of weight with me.

Well, I watched the three of them follow up that trail, talking softly to each other, all the way, until they come to the spot where the big, flat-topped rock was.

'Here the trail ends – try that rock,' said Grenville.

Then, in a minute I heard a deep chorus of voices, partly discouraged and partly excited; and I knew that they had found the place and they understood what it meant.

'Here's one stone – one diamond!' said Grenville presently. 'Some fox has been here before us. Now, let's find the man!'

XXI

Poor Old Daggett!

Well, I could have cursed myself properly to think that I had waited there until Grenville and his men came to that conclusion. If I jumped up and started running now, they would be sure to spot me; and, though it was a dark night, they had a spotlight to show them where to shoot.

'This way!' I heard Grenville saying. 'See how short his steps were! He was lighting matches, here, and looking at the loot.'

By this time I was working my way out of that clump of brush which had looked so good to me and so safe to me a little time before. I got into the clear, but it took me a terrible lot of time, for I had to feel my way along in the pitch dark, and treat every limb of the bush as though it were a bottle of nitro-glycerine.

But clear I was, at the last – and I got up on my hands and knees and sneaked off a little ways until

I thought it might be safe to stand on my two feet.

Just as I was about to sneak off at a run for the corner of the house, there was a sudden flash of light that fell across me from their spotlight.

'Mind your footing!' snapped Grenville.

But one of the others called in an excited voice, 'Did you see that? Who was that?'

'Where?'

'There! There he goes!'

I was up and away; but, as I jumped into full speed, their light steadied and shot full at me.

I dodged out of the path of it as I heard Grenville sing out, 'Willis! It's Willis! I might have guessed he would be on the inside when the crash came. Boys, if you down him, we are rich!'

They found me with that flickering light again, and three guns smashed at the same time. I felt a bullet knife through the upper part of my left arm; and then I turned the corner of that house a little faster than a running deer when the hounds give tongue behind it. They followed as fast as they could; but they would have needed wings to get me, after that.

I had intended to cut off toward the woods. But by the hot spurt of the blood down my side, I knew that I needed help, and that I needed it quick and bad.

I rounded to the front of the place, leaped up onto the porch, and kicked open the front door.

I slammed it behind me in time to have it splintered from top to bottom by two or three bullets. And at the same time I heard two voices shouting in the bottom part of the house; and then two guns sounded in quick exchange.

After that there was silence again. No one seemed to be stirring on the outside of the place. And on the inside there was a terrible dead silence for another moment – then I heard a faint groaning from the bottom part of the house.

Well, I glanced down to that arm of mine and I knew that I would have to find a friend and find one quick. So I put my head back and shouted, 'Lou! Lou Wilson! D'you hear?'

I waited another minute. A door slammed somewhere.

Then, 'Hello! Doc?'

That was the voice of Lou, and nothing ever sounded half so good to me as her voice when she was singing out. I went up the stairs three at a time; and I found her on the landing above. She grabbed me.

'What's happened? What has happened?' she gasped.

'I don't know half,' said I, 'but just now the main thing is for you to leave go of my left arm. It's been hurt and I want you to tie it up for me.'

'Here's the hospital,' said Lou. 'Come in with me!'

She took me into the same room where she had been sitting with Alston when things began to happen. Alston wasn't there now. But young Grenville sat in a chair in one corner of the room, slumped far back, his eyes closed, and a bandage tied around his head and passing over a part of his face. I didn't have to ask how he had got that. It was where the long, cold, heavy barrel of the Colt had landed when I knocked down the man who had been with me on the balcony outside of the window.

But Larry Grenville wasn't alone there. Lou was right in calling it the hospital. At the table there was a big hulk of a man sitting with his face in his arms, and his arms resting on the table. By the wide look of his shoulders I knew that it was Buck Logan. He raised his head. There was a bandage right straight across his eyes, and I guessed that Harry Grenville had been right when he said that Buck was blinded.

'What happened, Buck?' said I.

'Plenty,' said he, as cool as you please. 'How are things with you, kid? You'll have to tell me. I'm through with seeing for myself.'

'It's not as bad as that,' I told him. 'It sure can't be as –'

There was a little cry from Lou, here; because she had got my sleeve cut away and she was seeing the wound and the blood that was welling out of it. But she didn't make any fuss; she went right on like a brave girl, and begun to tidy up that wound, and then to put a dressing on it.

'It's as bad as all that, though,' replied Buck. 'I'm a gone goose, kid.'

'What happened?'

'I was down in the cellar, waiting till Alston had

scared old Daggett that way. And when he came, like a fool I let him see me. I forgot that he had a gun with him.'

'A gun loaded with blanks,' said I. I remembered the sound of the shot that Daggett had fired at Alston when that crook pretended to fall dead under it.

'Loaded with blanks, yes,' said Buck. 'But when a blank is fired close enough, what happens? Think of a cat spitting fire!'

Well, that was enough to tell me what I wanted to know. You watch the spurt of a Colt fired in the night and you know what I mean. The jump of the fire goes quite a little distance, and I knew that the burning grains of powder had spurted into the eyes of Buck Logan. I remembered, too, that the scream that I had heard from the bottom part of the house not long before old Daggett had come running out. And that was it! It was the yell of Buck when that torment was shot into his face. Enough to break even his nerve, though that was stronger than good-proved steel.

Well, I had had a good many doubts about Buck, but when I seen him sitting there so quiet and so calm, I had to put a hand on his shoulder and say, 'Buck, old-timer, I'm sure sorry! I'm mighty sorry! But the doctors these days can fix up pretty near anything; and they'll fix up you, too! Wait and see, you'll be all right.'

He smiled. Have you ever seen a man smile when his eyes was covered? Leastwise, with Buck, it was like watching the grin of a wolf.

'I've got what's coming to me,' says Buck. 'I don't whine. I'm finished. But when you get your arm tied up will you do one last thing for me, Doc?'

'Sure,' said I.

'Thanks. It'll be about the last thing that I got to ask from anybody, I suppose. But go down and find Alston. He'll be around in the lower part of the house, messing about. Get Alston and bring him back up here. But don't say that it's me that wants him. I got to have a talk with him. you hear?'

'Sure,' said I, 'and I'm fixed up fine right now!'

I got downstairs; and I turned to the cellar door, and through it I soft-footed for the cellar beneath, because there was where I was most likely to find Alston, according to what Buck had said. There I found him, too, being led to him by a faint glow of a lantern.

He was too busy with his work to pay any attention to me. He was working away at the wall, taking out stone after stone as quick as he could free it from the cement. And already he had cleared away enough to show a great gaping hole – a hole that led not outside into the night, but into a vacancy between the two walls that had been built there. It looked pretty ghostly; but I could remember how old Daggett had seemed to walk out of the solid side of the house, and I could guess what Alston was after.

And Daggett? I thought he was asleep, at first, for he lay on his back, stretched out so peaceful with his eyes closed. But then I seen the purple splotch at the side of his head, and something about the stillness and the stiffness was enough to make me understand – even though I hadn't stopped to think that he wouldn't be lying down here asleep on the cold cellar floor.

No, he wasn't sleeping. He was dead. I remembered the two shots and the groan. Alston must have done the rotten thing, though I couldn't see how even Alston could ever get as low-down as to do a murder like that one.

I slipped up behind him and put the cold mouth of my Colt against his neck. He sagged forward and drew in his breath with a bubbling sound.

'Get up, you coyote!' says I.

He waited half a second.

'Willis!' said he.

'Maybe!' says I.

'Curse the day that ever made Logan hire you!' says he. 'What do you want with –'

'Don't turn around, and put your hands up good and high. I sure like to see them that way – as though you was holding up the roof from falling. That's just the way I like to see you, old-timer.'

'All right,' says he. 'But why all the fuss?'

'I don't know,' says I. 'I was sent for you!'

'Did Logan send you?' he asked quick and sharp.

'No,' I lied. 'You've asked enough questions, and now I'll ask a couple. What happened to old Daggett?'

He didn't even bother trying to deny it.

'Silly old fool was stubborn. He irritated me too much. Where do you want me to go?'

'March ahead of me,' said I, 'with your hands up all the way. Poor old Daggett! I tell you, Alston, I'm aching and yearning and longing to kill you. I hope you'll give me a fair excuse. And I'll tell you this – you're the first man I've ever met that I'd as soon shoot through the back as through the face. You hear me talk?'

He heard me, and a little wriggle ran down his back as the chilly idea that I was all in earnest went to his black heart. Then he marched on ahead of me without a word.

I herded him up the stairs. And only when he come to the door of the room where the rest was, his eyes turned toward Logan, and he hesitated a little.

'Good!' said Logan.

But I looked chiefly at the girl, and her face was a study of disgust and contempt as she eyed Alston.

'Not even dangerous – to a man!' said she.

'Here he is, Buck,' said I. 'And now, old boy, what do you want with him? He's got his hands up in the air.'

'Oh, none of that! None of that!' says Buck. 'Him and me are friends for too long to need anything like that. I want him to sit down here close to me. That's all. Set him down in a chair close to me.'

I told Alston to do what was ordered; and, when he sat down, Buck put out a big brown hand and gathered in one of the wrists of Alston. And I seen a shudder go through Alston's body. He was a pretty sick-looking fellow, if ever I seen one.

'Gents,' said I, 'I dunno what's in the air here; but I got to tell you this. Here is Alston, the only uncrippled gent that we got left; and Grenville and his bunch are all outside and raving and tearing to get inside this here house because they know that the jewels of Daggett are here.'

'How do they know that? How do they know that?' snapped Alston.

'How do we know that they're here?' I asked, sneering.

'Forget about the jewels, Al,' said Buck. 'Hear me chatter, will you?'

XXII

Gun Play

'Well,' says Buck, 'I'll only keep the attention of you gents for a few minutes. I want to tell you about a couple of boys. One was a bad boy that used to punch the noses of the other boys in the school. And one was a good boy that was always at the head of his class and that was so smart that he knew how to have his fun and always shift the blame of it onto the head of the bad boy. And yet when there come a pinch, he always knowed how to make the bad boy his friend, and to use him.

'Buck –' says Alston, getting white.

'Never mind, old-timer!' says Buck. And he begins to pat and stroke the hand that he was holding. I felt that something pretty dreadful was in the offing, but I couldn't guess what.

'Well,' says Buck, 'the bad boy left the school. Run away – and he didn't go back no more. But a long spell later on, when he was a young buckaroo, he meets up with the good boy. Says the good boy, "There is lots of gold in the camps, kid. I'll go inside and work them with the cards. You stay on the outside and work them with your gang. I'll feed you the information that you need all the time. And you and me will split up the profits, understand?'

'Well, the bad boy thought that this was pretty good. He done the thing. The good boy played cards and got the information, and he passed it out to the bad boy; and the bad boy, he got into the swing of holding up gold shipments and having a good time all around. And being bad, he had fights. And being a steady hand, when he had a fight, he most generally did a little killing. You understand?'

Oh, I understood, well enough. We were hearing the inside history of Alston and somebody else – and the name of Carberry was the one that was behind my teeth. I would of given a lot of money to know how Buck come to hear all of this stuff.

'Finally they made a big pot,' went on Buck.

' "What are we gonna do with this stuff?" says the bad boy.

' "Turn it into jewels. They bulk down even smaller than bank notes," says the good boy, who had a pretty wise head on his shoulders.

'So they each turned their half into jewels, and they met up and counted over the shiners what they had collected and admired each other and the size of the pile that they had got together.

'The bad boy, he proposed a drink. And the good boy said that it was a darned good idea, and first he slipped a little pinch of knock-out drops into the booze of the bad boy.

'And after the bad boy had taken the drink, he gave a yawn and went to sleep.

'The good boy took all of the loot and disappeared. And the bad boy, he pretty near died from the effects of that stuff, because the good boy had meant to kill him with the poison; and nothing saved the bad boy from dying except getting powerful sick.

'Well, when the bad boy got his senses and his health back, he says to himself that he has been bad for a long time, and killed his men and done a lot of damage; and here he winds up in the end with a good chance of getting himself hanged, should the news of him ever leak out. But he decided that he would now try his hand at going straight. So he got himself a new name and a string of mules and started being honest. And he thanked Heaven that his face wasn't known, tied to the name of Carberry!'

The cat was out of the bag, now.

Alston gave a gasp and he says, 'You idiot, Buck – what do you mean?' And he reached back to his hip pocket.

'Steady, Alston!' says I. 'Remember what I told you while we was coming up the stairs!'

And I tilted my gun down and watched him through the sights – not a pretty picture, either.

Buck went drawling on, 'But after I had gone straight for a long time and begun to respect myself and the rest of the world, pretty much, along comes Alston and says to me, "Carberry, this is the time for us to make a grand clean-up. Point your gun the other way. It won't do you any good to kill me now because I tried to kill you and did rob you that other time. The thing for you to know is that the stuff I stole from you I lost afterward. And more besides! Your stuff, Carberry, and mine; and the Grenville jewels that I lifted and had along with me; and the gems I polished off a chap by name of Daggett! This here Daggett was about to lose his stuff through his wife – when he popped up, shot me down, and then went mad and lost the stuff where he himself couldn't find it. But I have the world's greatest scheme for making Daggett himself lead us to that loot. And a grand big fortune it is!" '

Alston put in with a sort of a scream, 'He lies! He lies like the very devil!'

'But in this deal,' said Buck Logan, alias Carberry, 'I've collected my finish. And now, Alston, you've come to your finish, too!' And as he said that he yanked at his clothes and brought out a Colt that looked about a yard long to me and black as a bucket of paint.

Alston screamed like a wild man and jumped up and snatched out his own weapon. He fired first, and Buck sank onto his knees, a dying man; but he still had hold of Alston's hand, though Alston was screaming and fighting to get away. And Buck dragged him closer and reached out his Colt until the muzzle of it got to the body of Alston.

Then he fired twice.

I got to him in time to knock up his hand after the second shot; but I was a long, long time too late. Alston dropped dead; and Buck sagged down on the floor, his big head wagging from side to side.

I forgot everything except the jolly old days when we'd followed the mules up the trail toward the valley. I forgot all the lies and the double crossing.

'Buck!' said I.

'Is he dead?' says Buck.

'Yes,' says I, 'and for the killing of him you pretty near deserve a reward, Buck!'

'The reward I deserve is what I'll get!' says he. 'Shake hands with me, kid. And remember this here one thing, will you – that the white man you knowed by the name of Buck Logan was white, though his name wasn't Logan, and –'

He died there, and I felt the strength go out of his big hand. But I couldn't see his dead face. There was too many tears in my eyes.

Which would prove that even a Carberry could be loved by a friend; but nobody on God's earth would ever dream of grieving for half a minute for that rat Alston. Or for any of his kind!

Now that Buck is finished, there don't seem much energy in me for telling the rest. Because, really, the rest was all happiness.

Before we left that house we had to make a dicker with the gang of Grenville – I mean that Lou and me did – that we would let the first sheriff be the umpire. The first sheriff was. He come and seen the house and he heard the story. He took the loot and groaned.

'Why wasn't I born to be a crook?' says he. And then he turned around and put me in jail!

Well, that was just his way of seeing that I got justice; and I sure had plenty of it before I got through. For five months they seesawed up and down, until they finally got it clear in their heads that I hadn't killed nobody.

By that time Lou and me was only waiting to get married. And by that time the jewels had been gone over. Larry and Henry Grenville were able to pick out the stuff that had belonged in their family. And other folks turned up here and there to make their claims. Yes, plenty of claims, and nine tenths of them crooked! But all that had any sort of proof got their stuff back.

And the rest – about a third of the stuff that we had brought in – was turned over to Lou and to me; and we made it a wedding present. She had her doubts about starting our lives on blood money; but I tried to convince her that she had no right to complain, because if it hadn't been for us, everything would have been lost to the world. And, to make amends for anything that was tainted in that coin, we made our decision to start right in where poor old Daggett had left off.

And that was what we done. It took ten years of hard work. It meant sinking money by the tens of thousands. But across that desert we run a road that nobody would be ashamed to travel on. And the railroad got interested and run up a branch line to the creek. And we cleared the big meadows; and we fed the big trees – or a handy part of them – into the sawmills.

I dunno that this here job has really paid, and I can figure out that if we had put the money out at five per cent in the first place, it would of done a lot more for us in the meantime; but, just the same, we never regret it.

Because, between you and me, we feel that old Daggett himself must know about what's happening, and that it would sure tickle him to see the valley prosper the way it has under us.

The old house is gone. There was too much sorrow in its roots, as you might say. And we put us up a big, rambling careless sort of a log house. But the kids like it, and we like it. And Daggett Creek comes winding and singing and shining right past under our windows. So what more could a body ask?